Victoria'

by

Jamie Penn

Chapter 1

Victoria had been in this predicament so many times before. No-one knew she was there and wherever she placed herself, they never would. The skills that she had taught herself and acquired from this had meant that her body had been kept trim; in order to remain able to watch whoever she wanted, wherever she wanted. She was like no other killer before her or since.

Sat in the child's playhouse as dusk settled in the garden of the Duckerton's, Victoria's lungs full with the cheap new plastic smell. It was supposed to resemble a real house but with windows that opened out. Even the door had a lock on it that she had been forced to lock herself so not to attract attention, as it had been banging against the house in the breeze. It had obviously not been used as it was in an immaculate condition and the stickers of flowers on the outside hadn't even begun to peel off yet.

There was a gaudy pink plastic table with matching yellow and pink plastic chairs set up inside of the playhouse, they were for the twin girls to pretend that they were in their own house, having their tea. Victoria wondering if the two girls should in fact re-enact what really happens at a dining table where they are not allowed to talk, make a mess, eat everything on their plate and never put their elbows on it. They were not going to be forced to stick to those rules at this table, but would have to obey them in the house. Double standards really.

Victoria looked through one of the four small square cut out windows in one half of the windows of the playhouse. There she saw that Mrs Duckerton was preparing the usual main meal of the day as she could smell something with a lot of garlic being put together. Almost every night that she had watched this family, the constant smell of garlic would waft from the kitchen windows and into the garden. It was a good job that she was not a vampire, otherwise she would not have been able to get near the house without her skin peeling off before she even reached the brickwork. The clattering of pots told her that it was almost time. It would be time to make her move when they were eating.

Victoria had the knack of moving and not making a single noise, even on creaky floorboards. It was something she'd mastered during her long stays in her Auntie's creaky, ancient mansion as a child. Not making a noise was something that was more of a necessity. Her lack of sleep would mean that she could wander the house seeing how long she could potter around without being heard or noticed. If her family knew how many times she had watched, literally inches from them as they slept they would freak out. There were never any urges or need to hurt, maim or kill any of her family whilst she would practice her silence skills. She loved them all and it would be worst thing in the world to lose any of them.

At the moment Victoria saw Mrs Duckerton carrying the plates into the dining room, she quietly exited the playhouse and looked at either neighbour's kitchen windows to check that no-one was watching. Moving stealth like towards the back window she crept up to it as it was still left open to allow the heat/smells waft out of it, it was way too easy for her.

The strategically placed boulder from the garden that she had placed underneath the window the previous night provided a makeshift step for her to stretch her body through the window, hardly touching any of the surfaces as she moved. Both adults in the house would just presume that the other had moved it there and forget to mention it to the other if they had casually spotted it had been moved.

From previous visits, she knew that the family would be sat at the dining table facing the wall, just as they did every night with their baby twins at either side of the table facing each other. Even if the babies were to see her, they would hardly raise suspicion and point her out to their parents. A peek around the corner of the kitchen revealed to her that they were tucking in to their lovely freshly prepared meal. The need for them to savour the food with every bite overwhelmed Victoria as she knew it would be their last. Brisk but silent footsteps allowed her to walk behind the family without even being spotted by either child.

As Victoria approached the front of the main lounge towards the stairs, someone knocked on the large oak front door. Luckily she had been alone in the house enough to know where was good to hide.

As the man of the house shut the door on the charity worker, the smell of the sweat coming from him and his body odour made her feel so good. The reason she had been attracted to this family in the first place was the smell of him. As he returned to the dining table Victoria continued her journey up the stairs and into the master bedroom. This place was so familiar to her now; she had seen it so many times and knew exactly where to stay to remain unnoticeable until the time was right.

At 7.20pm the couple brought the baby twins to bed; they had decided for their twins to have separate bedrooms and took it in turns to put them to bed each night. Behind the piles of clothes Victoria could hear the cooing noises and infantilization that was involved in the process of speaking to babies. It had been at this point on many a night; that Victoria had returned downstairs, hidden and watched as the Duckerton's had returned from their children, sat cuddled up on the couch for hours just watching TV and drinking. She had thought it tiresome, boring and a waste of their time; they could have been doing something far more constructive than that. The boredom of watching them cuddle had meant that the remainder of the evenings had been spent behind their clothes waiting for them to venture up the stairs. That is where the fun began.

Waiting for them to complete their bedtime ritual is one of the things Victoria really look forward to, it gave her an insight to what was important to people; this couple were just the same. Sometimes they would cuddle, other times make love and she would wait for them to fall into a deep sleep and others she could feel the tension between them after an argument or a disagreement that had not been resolved.

Tonight she watched and waited for the initial twitching to stop and the rapid eye movements and mumbling to begin. Tonight like every other night previously, she would climb down out of the open plan wardrobes from behind the clothes not making the slightest creak. This route had been perfected by performing it ritualistically during the day for weeks whilst the house was empty.

Victoria stood at the foot of the bed and watched as they slept holding each other, sharing their body heat after a session of oral sexual pleasure. Neither had cleaned their teeth afterwards which had sickened her slightly, but she wasn't going to be kissing them. In fact no-one would be from now on.

The weapon of choice sat in her hand and she unfolded it from its sheath. It glistened in the moonlight, shining through the uncovered windows. Victoria looked down at it and stepped up onto the bed with her left foot first. The wife was a heavier sleeper so her side of the bed would be easiest to rock slightly. She pulled her right foot up onto the bed, using her hands to make it a gentler landing, eased her fairy steps closer towards their waists. When she had positioned herself into the precise vantage point; she put her hand into her pocket, brought out the bottle and poured the liquid on a cotton wool pad.

Victoria squatted down, leaned over her and ever so slightly she rubbed the side of her neck with the cotton wool pad. Again, this was something she had done a few times before but without the liquid on it. She had been testing the woman's reaction to the feeling to see if it would be safe. After the application Victoria grabbed her weapon up from the bed sheets, finished counting to thirty and sliced her carotid artery; the anaesthetic doing its job to render the wound painless.

As the short bursts of blood channelled out of the wound; she turned to Mr Duckerton, pushed him onto his back using her right foot onto his left shoulder, and just as he was rousing she stabbed him through his chest cavity into his heart. He writhed around for a few seconds but the wrestling submission move Victoria placed on him straight after the impact rendered his battle useless. Even for such a slender, petite woman she had a tonne load of strength and her legs wrapped around his head and his arms stretched back behind him was enough to subdue any efforts he may have had. She positioned him so he could see the last remaining bursts of blood trickle from his wife's neck.

In her grips, Victoria could feel him losing consciousness just as the wound turned to a steady stream. After another minute of Victoria rubbing her body all over him, transferring his smell onto her, she let go of the submission hold, stood back up onto the bed and turned to look at the fitted wardrobes that she had sold them. She smiled and admired her work. These two like the others were less worthy than her, now they were in their rightful place.

Victoria walked off the bed and grabbed their house phone which was situated on the landing area. She walked into one of the twin's bedroom, the one she has grown fondest to whilst watching them and as she stood looking at her, she knew that what she was about to do would save them both from the disappointing vacuum of a life than if those two would have been left to raise them.

Victoria pressed the button to get a ring tone, dialled 999 and left the house the same way she had left on the other nights. Totally undetected.

Chapter 2

Victoria had an average upbringing. No abuse, no traumatic experiences from an Uncle or other male relatives. She went to decent schools and achieved higher grades than anyone who knew her thought she would. The family that she had were all kind, apart from the odd one that all families have and she never wanted for anything. Her parents always tried their hardest to get her anything that she wished for and had taken her and her younger sister on numerous holidays all over the UK and Europe. On her holidays within the UK she had loved beach holidays and the highlights including collecting shells, sitting in an amusement park playing bingo with her Mum and Grandma hoping to win the 50p cuddly teddy on the top shelf, making sandcastles and trying to stop her brother from knocking them down, looking for crabs preferably still alive, playing swing ball and listening to the collective urinating in the communal bucket in the five person tent that her Father had chosen.

At primary school she loved to play and do craft work. She was always good with her hands and sometimes had such an imaginative mind that a lot of her craft work was shown in the assembly at the end of week and even put into competitions within the local area. She never won any of them as the judges often thought that her parents must have helped her too much so she was always overlooked for the one that was 'obviously' done by a child. She had three or four best friends, depending on how many of them were talking to her at the time. Its so much different for girls at school with friends, the psychological blackmail that involves being friends at times is reminiscent with those of someone with revealing photographs of you that you will do anything to keep away from your family. Whereas boys just run about, fight, play sports and have no cunning in their heads at all. Well that would constitute thinking about stuff and they can't be bothered with that, if you are mates then great that's it.

Victoria loved playing hide and seek with her friends in the local abandoned school near her house, playing Monopoly and other board games with her family and the early computer games which she preferred to the more visually real games of today. There were many friends in her life; from the ones she made at primary school who would mould her ways of socialising, to the early boyfriends whose relationship with her were the boys who didn't say she smelt or had head lice. You know really romantic comments.

She watched TV like any other child and young adult, she was subjected to the slack restraints that her parents felt she could cope with at the time. Allowing her to watch programmes that others deemed not suitable for her or games that her mind would not be able to handle. She experimented with alcohol earlier than other teenagers do which had caused a few experiences that she now regrets but none powerful enough for them to damage her enough to kill for a reason.

Victoria's handwriting skills, English, mathematics and art work improved it seemed in every term until she eventually moved into high school. There were no traumatic experiences to talk of in high school either, apart from the obvious boy troubles that all teenage girls go through, the constant changes in hormones and the jealousy of the popular girl. That is until you reach a certain maturity when you find out that the popular girls are popular for all of the wrong reasons and it is girls like you that will end up happier than them in the future, instead of being known as the girl who wanked every lad off in the school just because he said she had nice tits or got help with her homework.

The friends she made in secondary school were all known as 'geeks' and 'nerds' plus her close male and female friends who she could immediately turn to and who would turn to her in hard times. She didn't mind the names they were called, she had been told by her Grandparents that geeks and nerds always found good jobs, whilst the bullies almost always syphoned the state for benefits and jobs that they would hate until death took them early from life. Little did she know that she would take people earlier no matter what kind of educational needs they had?

There was no cliché that a normal serial killer can attach to themselves to justify why she did these things. No boyfriends that beat her, no bullying that was bad enough for her to resent anyone in particular. She had not been subjected to any religion; that would force her to obey a fictitious lord who would punish you if you did anything bad to people, but then also punish you for doing good.

As she was of of the girls who 'blossomed' earlier than others, she found herself wanting to be more sexually active earlier than her friends. She loved the feeling of being penetrated and the fact that she could enjoy it for longer than other women, according to what she had read and spoken to older girls about. However, as she grew into a young woman and went to college and University, the men in her life could never keep up with her, so to speak, as she always wanted more from them while they were spent, asleep or just left after they had their way with her. She was almost always left unsatisfied, well apart from one man; but he was already taken and it was a drunken stupid one time thing she wished had never happened, but in the same breath wished that he would have been hers forever. Sadly it was never meant to be, there was no bitterness as she new he was already somebody else's and she would surely find someone who fit her bill again. Wouldn't she?

Eventually the whole sexual thing was not that much of a big deal to her in life when she had more important issues to bother herself with. She had a bigger purpose in life and one that did not allow her the time of such complicated relationships and all the explaining that comes with having someone close and killing people has. This she found out the day she had pushed Kelsey Starling over the footbridge onto the railway lines before the Hull to London train made her look like a crap butcher's window.

It was not a traumatic experience, it was a gentle push to someone who deserved it. The school bike who thought the way she would get on in life was on her knees, allegedly to one of the English teachers too as her grades were far higher than her outward ability. A girl whose rich parents had split and she made the most of getting exactly what she wanted. She hadn't caused Victoria any pain directly, she knew that her and her friends probably bitched about her, but she could handle that.

However, at that moment Victoria knew that everything she had been feeling over the last few months, all the conversations she was having with herself about being a superior person than the people who thought that they were, all of the thoughts that had been travelling around her head all met at the crossroads on that bridge. It was the first step in the direction should would be taking and she knew where she wanted to go.

As she matured, she enjoyed watching her pray for extended periods; pretending to be happy families and masturbating as much as she could in what she was seeing so she could enjoy the experience with them in her own way.

Victoria just loved the feeling of getting to know someone followed by viciously taking their life force away so she could feel superior to them.

She aspired to be the greatest predator that ever lived.

Victoria would prevail over everybody else, no matter who they were. This was her orgasm and she wanted to keep the feeling going forever.

Chapter 3

Victoria walked into work that morning at her usual part time hour of 10.30am. Her boss Martin had agreed these times after Victoria had persuaded him that customers didn't usually turn up until 11am at the earliest. To be honest Martin would do anything to keep Victoria working for him and even though she was wrong, customers usually come in at 10am how could he not bend around her arrangements? She was great with the customers, knew exactly what they wanted even if they didn't yet, she would go into the most minute detail of the bedroom furniture you would think she lived and breathed them. She was a very good saleswoman to both sexes and seemed to have the knack of persuading them to making the changes that would cost them more money but make it beneficial to them. This was of course beneficial to Victoria also as her job paid commission for the more money that the customer paid and even more if any recommendations to other local businesses, like the bed shop or bathroom fitters down the road ended up in a sale too. They all tried to look after each other, after all if one of them went out of business it would make a huge impact on all of them. Less people would visit the area = less customers. Simple really but not all businesses saw it like this. Entire blocks of shops all over the city had been closing for years since the large supermarket chains and big name stores starting setting up shop right in the middle of a once thriving area.

Victoria was petite at five foot four inches and was always dressed immaculately, in a very professional way for her job. She was not what the media would class and drop dead stunning but she was far from ugly. Victoria had something about her that attracted most people to her and her confidence was off the charts, just teetering on the brink of being conceited but not quite there to annoy people. She had shoulder length dark brownish hair that she always wore up on a bunch at work but came down the moment she walked out of the shop at the end of her working day. She had a petite body with small amount of curvature to it of any sort. She tried her best to make the most of what she had by purchasing specialised underwear and clothes that fashion magazines told her would accentuate her body to its fullest. She had always been this size from the age of eleven. Victoria remembers beginning secondary school and all of a sudden being the first one to start developing in her class. She had swaggered for a few months until almost all of the other girls had caught out and surpassed her whilst had she remained the same, apart from a small amount of growth on her behind and breasts when she was sixteen, but if you would have blinked then you would have missed it. Although like most women Victoria thought her arse was bigger than a blimp, yet this was the third feature that people seemed to notice and admire when meeting her. The first being her amazing hazelnut eyes that could pierce any heart of stone who had thought that they were not going to spend much money when they walked through the door. Second was her smile that could melt people into a state of mild confusion and just end up saying "Yeah" to any answer once they were lost in it.

Her arse however was one that made her laugh inside, every time that she caught someone staring at it when she turned around quickly to catch them but not letting the person know that she had caught them staring. She could never see the appeal, it is lets face it just a 'fatty pedestal at the top of your legs' as she used to tell Martin when the person she had caught staring at her had left the shop or if she had caught them on the way into work. Martin always laughed or smirked after she told him but knew exactly where everyone else was coming from.

Victoria had worked for Martin since returning to Hull five years ago. She had studied Criminology at London Metropolitan University but returned when she could not find any jobs that were suited for her. Returning to her family home had seemed the most appropriate thing to do until she found a job.

For two months she had to endure the indignation of signing on in the most depressing and soul vacuuming place on earth that was the City's job centre. She had only had to visit it twice but the trauma of both of those visits scarred her for life.

The first of the visits started with a walk along a long corridored room with workers at the edge of it and the dolites sat on settees in the middle, like cattle at a market. Just as she sat down, a woman from behind her desk begins to shout the name Ricky Johnson. She does this eight times without moving her rotund arse from her chair, you know in case he is deaf or hard of hearing. Victoria assumed that they would just sit and wait as there is nowhere to book in to say you are here, even though she had an appointment. Ridiculous & confusing to her, never mind the illiterate people who attend this place.

The rotund one has now stood up and is talking to a colleague wasting her time where this Ricky is. "Oh he might be here, try shouting again" she heard her colleague advise her. Victoria was visibly biting her lip, wanting to shout "WHY DON'T YOU SEE IF HE IS HARD OF HEARING AND IF NOT, HE ISN'T HERE SO, NEXT! but she refrained as then she would probably be made to wait longer or the tall, muscular security guard may place his Doc Martens so far up her arse, that she would be whistling his laces for the rest of the day.

As she stared into her smart phone she could already hear two desk clerks flirting and doing nothing. This had happened last time had the misfortune of coming to the job centre with a friend. Victoria sat there thinking, *Could you possibly stop looking at each others sexually attractive body parts until later and actually do some fucking work. Its a chore I know but at least you have a job. There were a dozen people sat waiting, okay they don't need to rush off to work or anything but they HATE being here. You can suck him off later love, just get us seen so we can leave as soon as possible and try and escape the gang of drugged up, alcoholic losers who stand outside all day and try to find a job. That would be a good idea now wouldn't it (that part was said in a patronising voice in side of her head, just like the one they use when you tell them you don't have a job).*

The chav next to me was looking at her. Victoria decided to put her smart phone in her zipped pocket and check where her purse was. He turned to her and informed her that she had to book in otherwise they won't know that she was there. Bless him, it has taken him four minutes to pluck up the courage to tell her that, or it had taken four minutes for his brain to send the information to his mouth. He showed her the desk that she had to go to and its the one where the lazy cow who was shouting Ricky was still sat. She was interviewing someone when Victoria had arrived so how the hell was she supposed to know that you had to book in there.

After she had told the woman her name, she looked around for any signs to tell you this. There were none. Dicks.
Victoria sat back down and thanked the chav, he did not respond but then he probably wasn't used to hearing compliments.

After that Victoria noticed how hot it had become in the room. It was either all of the hot air these gimps were spouting about there being plenty of well paid jobs out there or this is where our tax is going, to heat the job centre and make the unemployed even more uncomfortable. She noticed the security guard inch closer to a massive black bloke who had just walked in. No stereotyping there then is there, besides the security guard wouldn't stand a chance if he kicked off anyway.

One woman is working like a Trojan and has seen two people already and is on to the third. The rest of the people just sat staring into their pay slips, licking each others lips, probably on social media sites & laughing at the pogs as they sit there and roasted.

There were two men sat in suits opposite Victoria and a woman walked up to them and spoke about them being interviewed for a job soon. She had to laugh as they both looked down her top at the same time and then looked at each other. They then both checked her out as she walked away. The only thing that was missing was them high fiving each other. Now the staff behind of her began talking about Christmas shopping, Victoria's lips were about to burst as she was waiting fifteen minutes last time with her friend.

The sentence "aw it's out of order man" is spoken behind her as two dishevelled, pale looking scruffy gits walk past. They look like they have not eaten for weeks and they stagger out of the door. She looked around and noticed that there are lots of people walking about aimlessly. More people have turned up but no-one else's name has been called out.

Victoria noticed that one woman at a desk, on the right has been highlighting with her head down for eight minutes. It was then that she heard her name to be seen. She stood up, brushed her clothes down her body and walked over to the desk and her interview began.

She sat down and the woman asks if Victoria had written down all of the jobs that she had applied for, rang up about and been into shops for. "No" Victoria answered but before she has time to have a go, she informed her that she had found a job. The relief in the staff member's face was apparent and she could swear that she heard Kool and the Gang singing 'Celebration' in the background. She tells Victoria to keep signing on until her DBS clears then she can get what is entitled for her to receive, however she must come back for another interview in two weeks. When Victoria asked why, the staff member kept her hopes up by telling her that anything could happen in two weeks. A great way to keep her confidence up.

Two weeks later as she attempted to walk into the job centre with her spiced chai tea latte (which she was thoroughly enjoying by the way), she was halted and told that she could not take the drink inside and the security guard pointed to the sign on the outside of the automatic doors. When she asked why, he told her that it was in case she threw my coffee (its tea ignoramus) at a staff member.

It was then that she admitted to him that she was breaking two other rules too of the sign on the front door. Victoria told him that had a mint in my coat pocket and that she would be taking my mobile phone into the building as (and she knew it sounded stupid) but if she left it outside of the building whilst she was inside of it, it may not be there when she got back outside to collect it.

He told Victoria that she was okay with the mint and mobile phone, so then she asked why she could not take my TEA inside then. "It's the rules" he told her as he sheepishly walked away. Well he sort of thumped away from her as those security guards who double as bouncers do whenever they 'try' to walk.

As Victoria finished her TEA and walked back into the job centre, she walked past the same security guard placing the mint into her mouth with one hand, tweeting on her phone with the other and smiling like the Cheshire cat right at him.

Walking up the stairs (two flights of them this time) as the higher in the alphabet your surname is, the higher up the building you have to walk. She feel this may be a bit of discrimination to the Polish/Eastern European community as they will all have to go to the top floor. Actually, she suspected that the main reason for them marrying English people is so that they only have to walk up one flight of stairs when claiming their benefits.

Victoria went through the double doors on the floor where she was to sign in, but as soon as she had, she remembered that she had forgotten to take her signing on book.

"Have you brought your signing on book" the woman asked.

"No, sorry" she replied "but I was so desperate to beat the traffic having to come into town at Christmas shopping week that I have forgotten".

"Well, you must bring your signing on book otherwise you will not receive your benefits" she told her as she reached into her desk and brought out a slip of paper.

"Just fill this in please and make sure you bring your book in next time okay." Victoria filled in the slip of paper and gave it back to her.

"This is to make sure that you still receive your benefits"

"So, I don't need to bring in my book then"

"Yes" she replied and looked right at Victoria as the bouncer......sorry, Security Guard behind her began to shuffle.

"but if I do forget to bring it every time, I just need to fill in one of these slips?"

"Well yes I suppose so" and the pit bull's.......sorry, Security Guard's leash slackened again.

"Thank you, but I won't be here any more as I start my new job in under two weeks" and she walked over the seats that look comfortable, but make your arse hurt more than a pelican stabbing at it looking for food (just trust me).

There was only Victoria and a black lady waiting to be seen. They both nodded at each other, gesturing and greeting without actually saying a word. As she sat waiting she did not see any flirting, no highlighting of paperwork and someone had actually opened a window. They were different staff so maybe they were actually good staff or one of the 564 people who read her tweets after the last visit either worked there or knows someone who works there and told them about it. Victoria suspected the first instance, that was until she heard a discussion about Christmas knitting patterns.

She was about to tweet about it when she heard my name being called out. Victoria looked at the lady sat opposite me as she had been there before her and therefore should be next to be seen she would have thought.

As Victoria approached the desk, I shit you not, the woman behind the desk said "I was hoping it was going to be you".

Why was she glad it was going to be me? Not only are they discriminating to the Eastern European benefit scroungers by making them walk to the top of the building, they were now blatantly discriminating against this other lady who had been sat there longer than her and she was 'GLAD' to it was Victoria who she was seeing and not him.

She was probably still sat there poor woman.

Victoria signed another piece of paper that made sure that she received her benefits and left within two minutes of the woman's obvious racism.

As she walked back down the stairs past the first floor, two people walked out of the double doors and the 'woman' was informing the 'man' she was with that her benefits had now been halved. He whispered sweet nothings to her by stating "Well we won't be able to get enough gear this week then".

Victoria exited the building and decided to take the picture of what is prohibited in the job centre and that is when she realised the lengths this government is going to cut benefit fraud. It stated 'NO DOGS (EXCEPT GUIDE DOGS)'. However on her visits to the job centre she had seen many of them and the Security Guard had let them slip through too, BUT NOT HER CHAI TEA BLOODY LATTE!

A few days previous to her first visit to the job centre, Victoria's feet were kicking a stone along the path on one of her many long walks to halt the boredom, she happened to walk past a bedroom furniture shop on Spring Bank West that had a notice on the door looking for staff. She walked in, took the notice out of the window and asked to speak to the manager. She was immediately granted an interview and for the next forty five minutes she sold herself enough for Martin to think that he would foolish not to employ her. He has never looked back and despite the fact that he has tried to come on to her on three occasions, which she had brushed off, he knew she was the best thing that had happened to his business since he opened the shop seven years before she had walked in.

Other employees had come and gone but she had remained loyal and to the best of his knowledge, never looked for another job. The only thing she could not do was cover for him whilst he was on holiday. Martin had asked her, only to be told that she could not open the shop at nine in the morning or stay until seven in the evening to close it. Every time he is due to go on holiday, his other workers have to step up instead.

On the last occasion when he went on holiday; Carl the person who was covering for him disappeared two days before his return. He has still not been found to this day.

Chapter 4

Carl and Victoria had just finished their best week at the store without Martin there since Carl had worked there. The high five that they gave each other was truly awesome; knowing that they were excellent at their job, Martin would be so pleased and that the sales this week alone would keep the shop afloat for another four to five months.

They were on so much of a high that Victoria had even agreed to stay until the shop closed as customer after customer kept walking through the door, she knew that business would be lost if she left so she stayed with Carl until they eventually shut the shop forty five minutes later than it said on the door.

Carl turned the key in the lock and set the shutters off, slowly descending over the front windows of the shop. He turned around, looked directly at Victoria, the both smiled and walked towards one another. The walk became a short sprint but at the last minute Carl put his hand in the air, going for a high five. Victoria had completely misread the situation but still managed to recover enough to connect with her side of the high five in question.

After the sting of the high five wore off, Carl looked deep into those Hazelnut eyes and then came the cuddle. This was the first time in a long while that Victoria had been as close to a man in this position without her being in complete control. She could feel Carl's body pushing up against hers, not too intimately but enough for her to feel the outline of his body resting against hers. Even though he was half a foot taller than her, they appeared to fit together quite well. At this point Victoria noticed that the cuddle was going on for a few seconds longer than she thought it would. She looked up and there he was, looking directly into her eyes yet again, like he had been waiting for her to look up at him for the whole period of the cuddle. Carl's left hand moved from behind of Victoria and rested on the right side of her face, a few fingers on her cheek and the rest just slightly caressing her neck. Carl had to bend down slightly to reach Victoria's lips but meet them they did.

Victoria had always fancied him but had kept her emotions and feelings to herself as it would be too complicated. However, the moment he bent over to kiss her there was only one thing she could do, and that was to reciprocate. After the kiss they both stared at each other and she nodded to him. Neither of them could wait for the shutters to slam to the ground so they could lock up the shop. Even though it only took another forty seconds for the shutters to lock, it felt as if both of them were living in slow motion for a week. They locked the front door, put the shutters down, got into Carl's car and drove to Victoria's house.

On the journey, Victoria was assessing her house in her mind to see if it would be safe for Carl to view it. Thank fully Victoria was usually immaculate with her evidence hiding but it had been known that due to her having to straighten her hair, the odd morning had been known to be slightly hectic and her forget to put the odd tool away that should be hidden in case of a sudden raid.

The car stopped and they both got out. "Have you got any protection?" Victoria asked, only her actually knowing that it could be construed as a double meaning. "Yes I do but I don't want you to think that I was expecting it or that I always kept one for this purpose"

Carl answered sheepishly. "I just always have one as my Dad told me to always be prepared".

As soon as the door slammed closed behind them, Carl placed his hand on her cheek and turned her head towards his, he looked her deep into her eyes and kissed her passionately whilst stroking her neck. He could feel her embrace tighten as they kissed, his other hand now pulling her closer towards him too. Her hands were now stroking up his back and then pulled him closer by placing her hands onto his shoulders and pressing him against her.

Their tongues flicking against each others and they kissed in the rhythm that seemed like they had perfected over time, they even know where either one of them were going to rest and return to quick kisses. The passionate kissing ceased and she stared deep into his eyes with the look that he had fantasised about. The look that turned his legs to jelly and other parts of him to concrete.

He took her by the hand and guided her towards the back of the room and into the bedroom. They stood at the end of the bed and began to kiss again, after a short while he began to unclasp the back of her dress and then pulled the zip all the way down to the bottom. She grabbed his hands, stopped him and held his hands behind his back and told him to keep them there. She took a step back and lifted her shoulder straps up and then released the dress, allowing it to drop to the floor revealing her underwear. He could feel something say inside of his head "YES, GET IN!".

He began to move forward but she held her index finger up and shook it from side to side to tell him not to move. Instead she walked up close to him and she began unbuttoning his shirt. Once his shirt was fully unbuttoned, she slid her hands inside of it, caressing his chest and she slid the shirt over his shoulders and allowing it to join her dress on the floor.

She began caressing his chest and then guided her hands around his body and began to caress and scratch his back and then make her way back to his chest and stomach. His back arched with every stroke and scratch on it, then she reached down, moved his hands down by his sides and grabbed his buttocks and then dug her nails slightly in, over the material of his trousers.

The moan coming from him told her that he was ready. She held his hands in hers and then guided them up to her breasts. She placed his hands and her chest and the sensation that tingled from her nipples and all of the way up her chest made her so turned on that she would have happily let him take her there and then. She however had other plans, reached behind her back unclasped her bra and allowed him to remove it.

Her breasts now released from the bra, he crouched over, cupped her breasts and moved his face to her left and began to lick her nipple and tease the right one with his left hand. After a few seconds of him licking her nipple, he sucked and squeezed her breast and squeezed her right one as well and pinching her nipple between his fingers. The feeling of this made her reach down and feel how hard this was making him and she was more than happy with what she felt, so she began to stroke his cock from the base to the tip, up and down it becoming a longer journey with every stroke.

He switched breasts between his mouth and his hands; licking, squeezing, pinching and playing with even more intensity as he felt his cock growing harder. He moved his right hand down his body, past her stomach, pulled at the elastic waistband on her underwear allowing his hand them, make his hand down immediately parting her legs without him even trying to and he slipped his middle finger down the length of her pussy.

He could feel how wet she was and this only made him even more hard. That and the noise she made when he inserted his finger inside of her made his cock pulsate with such vigour she wanted it in her hand straight away. She unhooked his belt and unclipped it, unbuttoned the trousers and as she pulled the zip down her hand slipped inside of them as quick as it was opened. She squeezed his cock over his underwear and her hand immediately slid under the elastic and grabbed his bare cock in her hand.

He moaned and his legs turned to jelly, the only thing keeping him up with the grip she had on him. With her other hand she began pulling his clothes down and he didn't need any encouragement to help her do this as his other hand now had two fingers sliding up and down her pussy, brushing past her clitoris and then penetrating her pussy and sliding right inside her with each stroke.

As his clothes came off the bottom of his feet, she began to crouch down still grabbing his cock as she did. Now on her knees she looked up at him, her eyes as beautiful as the first time that they met (which he still remembers to this day) and as she guided his cock into her mouth, he could feel the vibration of her pleasure in doing this reverberate through the full length of his manhood and all of the way up his body.

Her still looking at him with that look she pulled back his foreskin with his cock still in her mouth and her tongue flicked away at the end as she guided his cock still further into her mouth. Her hand grasped the base of him as her mouth now ran the remaining length, in and out and flicking away the whole cock as she did. He grabbed the back of her head and got a handful of hair, as he did she knew that he wanted his full length inside of her mouth so she removed her hand and slowly swallowed his cock right to the base, squeezing her left thumb so as not to gag as she did.

When his cock left her mouth she stood up, grabbed his hand and pulled him onto the bed with him. He laid down on the bed, she removed her underwear and straddled his body so she could continue to suck his even harder cock, she wanted to feel his tongue on her pussy.

As her mouth gaped around his fat cock again, his fingers parted her and licked the full length of her now dripping wet pussy. The taste of her was amazing and this only made her want to lick her clit faster and with more energy as well as sliding his fingers inside of her as he did. He felt that he could lick her forever like this and all of a sudden felt the sensation from his cock that he was going to cum.

He told her and she laid on her back. In the time it took to move position her could feel the sensation subside slightly, so he crouched over her with his cock now at the level of her face. He guided his cock inside of her mouth and began to fuck her mouth, his cock filling her mouth with every thrust, her cupping and playing with his balls as he did. After a short while, he felt the sensation return and knew it was imminent, so he pulled his cock out of her mouth and as he came over her breasts he looked into her eyes and saw how much she was enjoying it.

Once his orgasm had finished and he had cleaned the cum from her breasts, he made his way down her body, kissing each inch of it on his way down. His lips caressing her stomach, past her waist and then the inside of her thighs, brushing past her pussy and he switches sides from one thigh to the other.

After a few times passing her wet pussy she begged him to lick her, so like the obedient man that he was he filled his full mouth over her pussy and licked the full length of her pussy, making sure that he licked every single millimetre of her, tasting her whole pussy as he did. Once he began licking and flicking her clit with the end of his tongue, he knew it was time to slide two fingers inside of her. Feeling her back arch and her moans become louder and more intense, he continued to lick her clit and pussy until he slid a third finger inside of her.

Hearing her being pleasured by him was making his cock grow hard again. He carried on licking, playing and sliding his fingers inside of her, occasionally using his thumb to play with her clit until she grabbed the back of his head, pushing his face deep into her pussy and she came while he licked her. He tasted her cum and she continued to pulsate as she orgasmed.

Once her movements subsided, he continued to lick her and play with her pussy until she told him to fuck her. He moved slowly up her body and grabbed his hard cock, pulled back the foreskin and rubbed his cock against her still raw pussy from her orgasm. She looked him deep into his eyes with the look he knew well. Once he saw this, he slid his cock into her waiting pussy and the noise she made, drove him further and filled her pussy full with his cock as he looked down on her as her face was filled with pleasure.

The feeling of his cock inside of her never felt any less amazing; the noises and looks she gave him as his cock was leaving and entering her only made him want to her to feel his cock get deeper and deeper inside of her. He spread her legs wider and placed them over his shoulders and plunged his cock as deep as he could inside of her and began thrusting as hard and as deep as his cock could reach. With every thrust he could hear her pleasure intensify and he slammed his cock deep inside her until she told him to fuck her from behind.

He reached down, grabbed her by the hips and swung her body around the bed, lifting her up onto all fours as he did. He felt her back with his right hand and stroked her from the base of her neck all the way to her amazing arse that was staring at him from below. He reached around and squeezed her right breast, as with the other hand he guided his cock inside of her.

Gentle motions to begin with as he pinched her nipple and squeezed her breast every time his cock filled her up, then he grabbed hold of her arse with both hands and began slamming his ever growing hard cock inside of her, with every thrust he she was screaming louder and louder, which in turn made him slam harder and harder and with that his cock became harder and harder. After a while, he reached forward with his left hand and grabbed her long red hair, he bunched it up in his hand and pulled. Together with his right hand now grabbing her right hip too, she could now feel all of his mighty strength, both in his arms and in his cock and she was being pounded like only he could do to her.

He could hear her screams becoming more prominent and changing and as his heard this, he felt the sensation that he was going to climax again. "I am gonna cum" he said, to which she replied "so am I" so with his right hand he reached around and being playing with her clit as he continued to pull on her hair and slam his cock deep inside of her until he came inside of her pussy just as she came all over his cock. He continued to pound her pussy until every drop was now inside of her pussy and so her orgasm could last as long as she wanted it to.

Once they both stopped moving, they both collapsed on the bed, his cock still inside of her. He reached over and grabbed the tissues that had already been strategically placed earlier and made sure they were clean before moving too much. Once that was taken care of, he laid pulled the covers back and laid down inside of the bed and when she returned from the en suite bathroom, she laid next to him, slung her arm over his chest, her leg over his legs and then pulled the covers over each other.

The snuggled for at least another hour; stroking and kissing each other, telling each other how amazing the sex had been. Neither of them had ever been with anyone before who they felt were so in tune with their sexual needs; never mind their physical, psychological and social needs too. They fell asleep in each others arms.

In the morning, Carl woke up and went to make him and Victoria breakfast. Ten minutes later Victoria reached over to feel for Carl's wonderful body that had pleasured her so much the previous evening and night; but he wasn't there. A head rush followed from her rising out of bed up so fast. She jumped out of bed and ran around the top floor of her house. Carl heard the commotion from the kitchen and came to the bottom of the stairs to see what was happening. "Are you okay up there?"

"Oh you are down there?" she snapped, realized her tone and changed it immediately. "I was worried that you had just left without saying goodbye" sidestepping and ignoring her previous tone of voice.

"I am down here making you some breakfast. Well as best as I can with what you have got".

"It's okay; I don't usually have breakfast but will have some if you have made it. I will be down in ten minutes, I'll just sort myself out."

After a lovely breakfast they both made their way to work, opened the shutters and before unlocking the door, they kissed in the back of the shop. The first customer through the door as Carl opened it couldn't help but notice that he was happy about something, the obvious bulge in his trousers told her that. It also had a positive outcome of the decision to buy the bedroom suite as long as he came and saw it after it had been fitted. It was a stipulation that obviously had Carl wondering why but agreed anyway because it was a sale.

As the day ended Carl wanted to meet up with Victoria later on but she had brushed him off as she had other plans. The plans involved the Kennedy's who she had been watching each night for the past week, apart from last night obviously, and she needed to restart her observations so she could rid the world of those less worthy than her.

Carl must have asked seventeen questions why she would not meet him as he did not like sixteen of the answers. The seventeenth answer was more of a response "Don't fucking stifle me Carl; we shagged each other once and spent the night together. Stop getting clingy already, let's take it slow" she had snapped, as her shift ended and she was walking out of the door.

How was she to know that he would see her later on?

Chapter 5

Laid flat in the back of the Kennedy's wardrobe, Victoria waited for them both to get back from work about 9pm and come straight to bed. She knew that they worked away for a door to door sales company, knowing this from the conversation she had with them when they had bought the furniture. They had always arrived home together, checked the downstairs was secure and then come to bed. This happened on every week night, which tonight was.

A weekend night was much busier, as the Kennedys usually had all of their friends over for what can only be described as an uncontrollable piss up. Victoria must have seen no more than seven couples soil the Kennedy's sheets on one night, no shame that everyone else was downstairs probably more than aware that this was happening. Victoria didn't even know if the couples entering the room were actual couples or put together by a fruit bowl and some car keys.

At 9.34pm the Kennedy's station wagon pulled up onto the drive, car doors slammed and the front door opened. As soon as the house door closed the shouting began, she could hear that the argument was about a sale that had fallen through that day. He was blaming her for being too vicious in her pitch and she was telling him that he was a pussy. A great intellectual argument I think you'll agree. He did not appreciate her every response telling him that he was a pussy. She was like listening to an assertive teenager with only one come back line. He was becoming more and more irate with every mention of the belittling feline insult, to the point where he stormed up the stairs like he was wearing boots that got heavier with every step and laid on top of the bed fully clothed.

"Shall I sleep down here then, Just like the gentleman you are!" came from the bottom of the stairs.

Victoria saw him shoot up out of bed like someone rising out of a coffin with purpose and almost ran down the stairs. "You go upstairs then you childish fuck!" shouting at her.

This wasn't going to end well and Victoria was worried that one of them may take this too far and spoil her planned fun. "Don't you talk to me like that Mark, I was only winding you up!"

"We have both had a bad day and we need to calm down and start again tomorrow, okay?" with a more composed pitch in his voice.

"Maybe we need to unwind" and the sound of glass being chinked was the next thing Victoria heard. She looked around her neat little space that she had created on the plans and came up with a good idea for the next one.

The drinking didn't last long, Victoria had expected that coupled with a long day & alcohol, it wouldn't be long before it would effect them. The couple walked upstairs together and as she began to undress, she walked over to Mark and pushed her breasts in his back. "Not tonight Sam, I am both too wound up and tired" he said with the sound of defeat in his voice "I don't think I could manage to, but hopefully tomorrow will be a better day." He turned around and kissed both breasts and began to undress too. Sam walked away like she had been the last one chosen for a team, sullen and with her head drooping towards her nightdress that had placed there neatly folded at 5am this morning. She put her nightdress over her naked body and clambered in between the bed sheets and faced the wall, away from Mark.

Mark was none the wiser of these non-verbal offerings as he was in the bathroom making the weirdest toilet noises Victoria had ever heard. After seven minutes he finally emerged, walked to the side of the bed, scratched his testicles and climbed into his side of the bed laying on his front. Victoria stared at them laying in the letter K position; Mark on the left and Sam on the right.

When she knew the time was right, in the fashion she had perfected she descended from her constructed hidey hole and lifted the valance up at the end of the Kennedy's bed. Victoria knew that they would never check under there as they were always in too much of a rush to do anything but getting to sleep. Trust this night to be different, but the outcome had been the same. She pulled out what she had stashed and as quiet as a mute mouse, she assembled what she needed.

The injection just below Mark's tendon in his ankle will have only felt like a slight tickle or a scratch, and even if he awoke he would only have three seconds to do anything about it, which he didn't. Victoria moved towards Sam with the stolen home made mask and canister, placed the mask ever so slightly over Sam's face and released the ketamine into her face. Sam's eyes opened and for the split second that she saw Victoria, or the parts she allowed her to see, would have definitely haunted her if she were had survived the night. Now both were completely under her control just the way she loved it.

Victoria returned to the foot of the bed and grabbed what she needed, walked up on the bed, turned Mark over, straddled his prone body and began. The symbol she etched into his chest with the box knife was one of a clock face with a snake eating itself on it. She had spent weeks trying to perfect the picture as she was never really gifted the skills to be an artist but was happy with the finished product. Victoria leaned back and with her left hand she sliced Mark's right wrist next to her left leg, swapped the knife into her other hand and sliced Mark's left wrist next to her right leg. She could feel the warm blood against her legs through the suit. It felt so good that it made her feel better than any man or indeed she had in any sexual act she had participated in. She remained straddling him until the flow of the blood had dissipated, and turned her attention back to Sam.

Victoria sat on the floor next to Sam, staring at her face with the crows feet wrinkles at the side of her eyes and the ones beginning to form on her top lip from smoking for twenty years. They looked like the folds in curtains when they are pushed back too far. Victoria opened Sam's mouth grabbed her tongue, pulled it out as far as she could and smeared the Botulinum covered pad onto it. Now Victoria knew that alone would kill her but she wanted to leave her mark on her, so she grabbed the knife again dug it into Sam's skin just underneath her right ear, grabbed hold of her hair to readjust her head and sliced underneath Sam's jawbone, across her neck and up to the other side of her face underneath her left ear. Victoria let go of Sam's hair, stood up, picked up the bag full of her toys and looked at them from the foot of the bed.

She knew that she had let them off easier than others she had killed but the end result remained the same and the satisfaction was just as overwhelming to her. Victoria turned around like a soldier on parade, walked out of the bedroom glancing at where she had laid so many times, down the stairs and opened the front door.

Walking to the end of the footpath she noticed a familiar vehicle parked outside. Carl wound down the car window and waved at her but as she got closer his facial expression changed from the clothes she was wearing. As he tried to wind the window up as fast as he could, like lightening Victoria reached into the bag, grabbed another needle, pierced Carl's neck with it and plunged the liquid into his system. Another six inches and Victoria's arm would have been trapped in the window, but again she had succeeded.

She unlocked the door from the inside, opened it and pushed Carl into the passenger side, which she made look easier than it should have been. The car's engine started up and she drove him to the only place she knew would be safe.

No-one came to this place any more; it was on the banks of the river Humber and the company that had previously owned it had left it derelict two years ago. She had heard that the area was in the pipeline to be a new shopping complex but the local council were having to argue about how spending that much money would justify its development. Victoria secured Carl to the passenger chair and waited for him to wake up.

As Carl roused from his induced state, the last memory he had flashed into his mind and he began to wriggle violently and scream. Victoria knew that no-one would hear him so she waited patiently for him to realize that and spoke.

"Why did you follow me?" was her first question to him.

"Wha…." smacking his lips to try and get some moisture back into his mouth "Um…what the hell are you doing? Let me go!" he shouted.

"You aren't in the position to be ordering anyone about, especially me now are you? Your tiny jealous, besotted mind couldn't let me just do what I wanted to do tonight and then see you tomorrow could it?" Carl didn't answer; he just stared directly into her eyes.

"Did you think I was fucking someone else?" and Carl just nodded. "Well I wasn't, I was ridding this world of two less significant individuals than myself. You see I have a lot of work to do and people like you just get in my way all of the god damn time. I have tried to stay away from such pathetic rituals as liaising with others, this just acknowledges why I do."

Carl sat completely in silent shock with what was exiting the mouth he had kissed last night.

"You have ruined a perfect night for me and I can't allow you to continue. There is only one way this can be rectif..." and was finally interrupted.

"Why are you doing this?" was the only thing Carl could think to say.

"Because there are far too many people out there that think they are worthy of sharing the air I breathe, but they are just futile sycophantic polluters that deserve to have their existence terminated."

"Let me join you" Carl announced.

This was not at all what Victoria had expected to hear and it actually made her stop and think. The two of them could create such perfect scenarios together, completely under the nose of Martin and the unknowing customers.

"Do you realise what that entails?"

"Yes, I would do anything for you" and she knew after that statement that she was being deceived.

"Okay, but if I come over there and untie you, you had better not try anything" she warned.

"I won't, I will succumb to your superior existence."

Victoria almost vomited at the sheer will of him trying too hard. She opened the driver's door grabbing the tool as she closed it, walked over to passenger side and cut the restraints that was holding him into the seat. Carl stretched and got out of the car. He walked over to Victoria, holding out his arms to welcome her into them. She walked away and stood at the edge of the embankment, looking out onto the River Humber.

"How are we going to do this then?" she asked turning to face him. As she did, she could feel him grip her right forearm. Victoria knew where this was going; she used his momentum and flicked her body off the floor reversing the twist on her arm he was about to perform, wrapped her legs around his head, grabbed both of his arms around his back and tensed up all of her muscled until Carl's body fell to the ground with her still attached to him like an anaconda with her prey.

Victoria grabbed Carl by the legs, laid him in the shallow waters of the Humber, slit every artery she could see and pushed his body into the open water. She walked back to the car and got inside. It had to be found nowhere near his body so she drove it to an estate known for its high level of crime and threw a lit pad into the already alcohol soaked seats. As she walked away calmly, still wearing her murder stained clothes, she smiled that she had again been victorious and that no-one could stop her.

Chapter 6

Victoria sat in the back office with Martin waiting for a customer to walk through the door. It was raining outside, not the rain where people still don't mind going shopping. It was the type where you have to be equipped to visit Atlantis to stop your bones from getting wet.

Thankfully in times like these the staff at 'Bedrooms 4 U' had contingency plans to past the time and relieve the boredom. They played eye spy, which in a bedroom shop became samey very quickly, they had a TV with a budget Freeview box attached to it but the problems were both getting a decent signal and putting up with mind numbing daytime TV. They also had Monopoly which Martin always cheated in.

The thing they usually chose was to log on the work laptops, design newer more outrageous bedrooms then send them to the warehouse and fitters to see if their designs were possible. They could spend hours coming up with designs, only to be told that they were not viable. This always frustrated Victoria as the only reason she did this was to carry on her vicious ways. She would design wardrobes with hidden compartments but not tell the people who were buying them that they were there. 'An extra panel for aerating the clothes so they do not become damp or more susceptible to creases' was another good way she got around designs.

The door opened and two men walked into the shop. Victoria noted that they did not look like a gay couple (because she seemed to know what a gay couple looked like, yes really) so they must either be brothers looking for a bedroom; no, fitters coming to eye up the latest designs; no they never do that, or they must be the Police. Her third choice was correct.

"Could I speak to the owner of the shop please?" the first and more rugged man asked.

"Yes of course" Victoria replied and went to collect Martin, who had already heard the request and was on his way to greet them.

"Can I help you Sir"

"Yes, well I hope so, I am DI Atkinson and I have come to follow a lead about a double murder."

"A murder?"

"A double murder yes, could we go somewhere to talk?" emphasising the double.

"The shop is empty and I doubt anyone will be in soon, plus we can talk in front of Victoria, she is my partner in crime" dry gulping at the stupid words that he had chosen.

"Er, I mean partner....in the business....here" the two Detectives looked at each other and laughed.

"Okay then Sir but would you mind locking up until we are finished?" Victoria grabbed the keys from behind the till and locked the door. The all sat down on two beds facing each other and the Detective begun.

"We are here because a couple were murdered and few weeks ago in their beds and they had recently purchased the furniture from this shop. Now all we need are the names of the men or company that you hire to fit your furniture so we can eliminate them from our enquiries."

"Certainly, we use Nobel and Sons, they have a warehouse off Witty Street. I'll get you their number if you wish."

"No, that won't be necessary Mr?"

"Newton, Martin Newton" and held out his hand to shake the Detectives which he reciprocated with a wry smile at the cheesiness of him.

"Do you remember this family coming into the shop? Wallace, show them the picture." His partner opened an envelope with a picture Victoria knew well. It had been front and centre on a mantel piece about a fire place. Both Martin and Victoria looked at the picture in great detail but looked like they didn't remember them.

"The babies are twins and they purchased the furniture two months ago" Detective Wallace announced.

"Ah yes" Victoria stated "I remember the twins, let me go through our records."

"There's no need for that, we just wanted to know if you remembered them. We already know they bought it from here" Atkinson informed them.

"I haven't seen this in the local paper or on the news" Martin said, speaking up.

"No, we are keeping it quiet for now so we would like your co-operation in that matter" Atkinson replied.

"Of course" Martin agreed and Victoria just slightly nodded.

As the Detectives left the shop, Martin picked up the phone and began to dial.

"What are you doing?" Victoria asked.

"Ringing the Nobels."

"Put it down now" and he did "If you let them know before the Detectives turn up, if there is a killer there you will give them a head start."

"Oh yeah, I wasn't thinking."

"And if they find out you had rang them, you would look like you are in on it too."

"It's just awful isn't it?" A poor couple murdered in their beds" Victoria saw a pause in his thought and he continued "They never said anything about the twins did they?"

"No and I can't believe that this hasn't been on the news."

It was at that point when she suddenly realised that only her first three kills had received any media attention. She didn't read the local newspapers or watch the news on the TV as she found it totally and equally brainwashing and mind numbing. However, now the realization that all of her work was not getting the attention it deserved was, to her absolutely unacceptable. Maybe she would have to try harder and make more on an impact to get the recognition she deserves, albeit in an unknown capacity.

On the walls of a room in the Police Station, hung by multi coloured tacks were over a hundred photographs of Victoria's kills. From the very first kill where it had almost killed her, right up to the Duckerton's. There was also a web of lines which tried, in its attempts, to puzzle things together that made no sense.

Chapter 7

The floor of the room had been cleared of hair that had been pulled out over the last two years, sweat that had been strewn across it and blood remnants that had seeped through footwear from all of the work done to try and catch the most vicious, sadistic and ferocious murderer that the city of Kingston upon Hull had ever come across.

Detectives Nick Atkinson and Tom Wallace were the third set of Detectives that had worked this case. The first set, Detective Foster and Gallows had retired not long after the first case. The file was place in a box, in a store room at the bottom of a very long corridor when no clues, motives or even suspects could be found. The person being an eighty seven year old spinster whose all remaining close relatives had died, no friends and no associates. She only had ITV to keep her company as her aerial only picked up the one channel. There were no prints, hairs or DNA markers to pin point any particular person, so with no relatives to argue that no-one was doing anything about it, the case was left cold.

Only when two other Detectives; Marcus Grant and Thomas Willington picked up the next case of a young married couple of late teen age being murdered in their beds, did Victoria's exploits start to get investigated again. No-one linked the first case with the second as it had been forgotten and almost seven months between them. There were little pointers that could have matched them together but none that would stand out enough to firmly match the two.

Detectives Grant and Willington also covered the third murder three months after the second. Another couple in their mid-forties had been murdered in their beds with different wounds but similar access/egress to and from the property. Again no traces of a killer could be found but before the Detectives could thoroughly get their teeth into the cases, they were both killed in a ten car pileup on Clive Sullivan Way (a stretch of motorway named after a Cardiff born rugby league player who had played for both Hull FC and arch rivals Hull Kingston Rovers) three weeks after the third set of murders. All three of these murders where televised and reported on in the local news, not so much the first as it only warranted a page fifteen couple of paragraphs story, but the other two were quite well covered by the media. However when Detectives Atkinson and Wallace were called out to another murder scene almost exactly three months after the third kill, Wallace immediately noticed similarities from the previous two cases that Grant and Willington had been responsible for. The couple found were two people who were having an affair at his house whilst his wife worked nights shifts and her husband worked away on the oil rigs. After the Detectives had spoken to their superior and got him to pass the previous two cases onto them too, taking them from two of the most experienced Detectives in their station, they immediately saw the comparisons to their current murder case.

From that day on, not one media representative had been allowed to report on the following murders in fear of being arrested themselves. After the fourth set of murders which the only suspected three were linked, there had been five other murder scenes to deal with almost every two months for the next ten months. Nine cases all together (ten if you included Carl) but Atkinson and Wallace only had knowledge of eight of them, the other still festering in a box. If only they knew what lay inside that box or at the bottom of the River Humber, it would blow the whole case open and Victoria would be a suspect in a matter of hours.

Nick Atkinson, Tom Wallace and his team of computer geeks, administrators and foot patrollers where all gathered for the usual morning briefing. Some staff had changed from the original group who had sat down ten months ago to be informed that Hull had a suspected serial killer on the loose. This morning was led by Detective Wallace who informed the team that they wanted all members of Nobel and Sons background checked for any crimes, misdemeanors or cautions. They were also interviewing them one by one today to hear all of their stories.

They were told that if they spoke to any of the workers, they were only to mention the case of the Duckerton couple, no others. The Detectives did not want even the slightest hint that there may be a serial killer on the loose in Hull. They were both from Hull and knew what the people of this City would do until the real perpetrator had been caught. Previous killers had been hunted down and the slightest sniff of someone being a suspect had resulted in that person being almost kicked to death and their families hounded and forced to flee the City. As the room emptied and the staff all took up their collective duties, Atkinson and Wallace stayed sat in the meeting room.

"Do you think one of these employees is the killer?" Wallace asked "because if they are, we are going to be asked why we haven't come up with this before now."

"I know but there has been just so much frustration with the lack of evidence hasn't there? We have tried so hard by pulling up the interiors of the house apart to find even the smallest amount of evidence. If it wasn't for Joyce in forensics noticing that all of the furniture was bought from the same company, we'd still be without a lead."

"I know, I just feel like either of us should have picked up on this sooner. It's staring us in the face really."

"Let's just be thankful that it has been spotted now and get our questions ready. This is gonna be a long day so I hope you brought the Tangfastics and strong coffee."

The day was indeed long as both Detectives left their jobs at 10.15pm. Two of the workers did not have alibis for the night the Duckerton's were murdered but one of those had interested both Detectives more than the other. He was called Stephen Wetherall, he lived alone, his family had appeared to have disowned him, had no social or love interests and spent every waking moment not at work watching TV programmes like CSI.

Atkinson and Wallace had spent two hours just talking to Stephen but had to release him as it was a voluntary interview and had nothing to pin on him. However, it hadn't stopped them put an officer outside of his house to watch him overnight. At 6.48am the officer watching Stephen's house watched as he walked past his car and into his house. The officer hadn't seen him leave but here he was returning with a carrier bag in his hand. He text Atkinson and Wallace what he had just seen and immediately answered a call from Atkinson.

To say that he wasn't happy was an understatement, but that unhappiness would manifest a thousand fold when the news of another murder scene was called in at two o'clock that afternoon.

Chapter 8

Mr and Mrs Rowbotham were both local entertainers, trying their best to break into the entertainment industry. They travelled the country as a double act with their show named 'Formidable', a mixture of mind reading, mentalism and magic. They had been to visit Victoria at the shop about eight months ago to ask about purchasing a new bedroom. Victoria had suspected that both of them at one point had tried to flirt with her and also tried to get the furniture cheaper by planting mind tricks in her head. These techniques did not work on her as she has found out from a previous experience on a stage when she was nineteen years old. The hypnotist had tried to get a line of people on stage to walk about like farm animals whenever they heard the noise of a tractor. The technique had worked with all but two, Victoria of course being one of them. The hypnotist had spoken less than kind to both of them, and ordered them off the stage with his hand over the microphone.

Something along the lines of "You cunts could have played along like the rest of them."

The duo had just performed their show for the last night of their run at the Hull New Theatre, an honour for anyone local to Hull to play. Other venues they had played at throughout the country had been more well-known but, to them a stretch of shows at Hull New Theatre was a dream come true and a reminder of when they had seen Derren Brown perform there on many occasions.

The stage door opened and out they stepped into the cold air on Jarrett Street to be met by a couple of dozen loyal fans who followed them all over the country. Victoria, who had been down the street waiting for the stars to emerge, started her car and drove as quick but as legal as she could to beat them returning home.

One of the fans approached Liam and asked if he would sign her thigh, which Liam replied "Of course, anything to please my fans" and he winked at the young adoring woman. The partner of the young woman had his picture taken with Hayley and gave her a pinch on the bottom after it was taken. Now usually Hayley would have hit out at such brazen behaviour from a stranger but after she spotted the wink she felt it was fair game.

As soon as the duo got into their car, the eruption began.

Victoria could hear the remnants of the argument as they got out of the car and both doors slammed. She sighed at the amount of times she lay waiting, an argument or a disagreement would spoil her proceedings and she would have to postpone the kill for another night. The front door opened and the noise from the now revved up heated discussion had turned into the time Liam had thought Hayley was about to leave him for another magician. This magician had been in the same social circle as Liam whilst studying and had become more famous in a shorter space of time. Of course Hayley would never leave Liam as he was her everything and he continued to genuinely amaze her every night with new little bits of the act that he would try out.

"All I am saying is that if we are really nice with our fan base, they will tell, tweet and Facebook their peers how good and nice we were, making it easier to become more famous and get what we deserve." was the end of the conversation Victoria heard as Hayley had decided not to answer that statement. The couple must have sat in silence for a good twelve minutes when all of a sudden Hayley piped up with.

"Well if you aren't going to apologise, I am sleeping in the car"

"You can't sleep in the car babes. If you are that cross, I will sleep down here and you go upstairs"

"No" Hayley replied, sticking to her guns "If you don't feel the need to apologise for winking at a fan after signing her thigh, then I am sleeping in the car."

Victoria heard Hayley rushing up the stairs, rifle through the bedding in the next cupboard, literally inches away from her, grab some, return downstairs, take the car keys, open the door and locked herself in the car.

Liam looked on out of the front door at his wife sat in their car trying to get comfortable and snuggle up with a duvet in a Vauxhall Astra. He walked over to the car, knocked on the window and told her to come back into the house. After a dozen knocks and being ignored; Liam turned around, shut the front door, locked it and went to the drinks cabinet.

Five decent sized tots of finest malt whiskey later and Liam was ready for bed. He peeked out of the window and saw Hayley still in the car but not moving. He knew she could get to sleep easily, but in a car was a new accomplishment. A mumble of some derogatory comment left his mouth but it was the whiskey talking and he made his way up the stairs.

It was 2.13am and to say that Victoria's patience was wearing thin was an understatement. The thought had crossed her mind to leave it tonight but these bastards had kept her waiting so she was going to make them pay. At 2.36am Liam was fast asleep, she crept out of her hiding place and almost hovered over the floor to where he was asleep in bed. Curiosity got the better of her and she made her way out of the bedroom, down the stairs and into the front room. Victoria moved the curtains to one side and looked out of the window. Hayley's body appeared to be curled up in the passenger seat and sound asleep.

Victoria returned upstairs with the deathly silence she had perfected and returned next to Liam's almost semi-conscious state. The stare she was giving him would have probably scared him death if he had awoken, tilting her head from one side to the other and licking her lips. Her right leg bent at the knee closely followed by her left as she knelt gently next to him, opened her bag from under the bed and got out the handcuffs. These were the handcuffs without the chain in-between them, these had the solid black metal bar refraining any movement whatsoever.

The needle with pancuronium bromide entered Liam's veins via his inner left elbow crease. The paralysing effect would last for a while but the handcuffs were a 'just in case' alternative. Victoria could slice his throat to silence him quite easily if the chemical ran out mid kill, but the security of the handcuffs would make the action even easier. The good thing about pancuronium is that the person can be a feel everything that is happening to them but cannot do or say anything about it.

One set of handcuffs came out of the bag as Victoria grabbed Liam's right hand and fixed it to the head rest. This action awoke Liam from his slumber but, as though he was in a nightmare, he could only look at what was happening to him. His left arm arose with this person gripping it, attaching it to the headboard with handcuffs. It was then that he noticed that his other arm was also cuffed there too but he could not feel them. His eyes darted back to Victoria, whose figure glistened in her kill suit. Whatever little curves she had, this suit showed them off perfectly. The fact that she was completely naked underneath was more than visible as he scanned her whole body.

A string of stinging nettles made their way out of the bag like a conjuror's trick with multi coloured handkerchiefs. The more Victoria pulled at them, the more became visible to Liam. When there was a sufficient amount in her hands, she laid them all over Liam's all but naked body. He could feel them bristle over his skin and hoped that is where they remaining, he was wrong. With a lunge Victoria rubbed the nettles into Liam's skin like a mother does with a rolling pin, ensuring the pastry is a thin as possible.

The screams from the stings never materialised but the pain definitely existed, he could feel each and every one of the stings entering his upper torso. Liam watched as Victoria stood, bent over her evil bag of tricks and rose up with a thick piece of string and a pair of scissors. The smile beamed on her face, only visible to Liam by the eyes was no even more unsettling for him to see.

Her hand again brushed the nettles as it made its way to his bedtime boxer shorts. With the far three fingers on her right hand, Victoria pulled down the boxers, exposing Liam's manhood. Knelt either side of his legs she held out the string and pulled it tight, made a small knot that Liam knew well and when she pulled it, the knot disappeared. The string was again held out tight but this time Victoria lowered her arms and tied the string around his genitals, pulled the string as hard as she could until his penis and testicles were visibly darker even in the dark.

He noticed her tying yet another knot three times, he knew these ones would not pull out and as the makeshift weapon came into view all Victoria could see was Liam's mouth gaping as wide as it could in an attempt to make any noise possible. As she sliced the base of the crumbled set of genitals, his unsheathed testicles fell onto the bed with a blanket of blood surrounding them.

Liam watched as she got back down from the bed and returned to her bag. This time when she rose, he knew he didn't have long left. For in her hand was the shiniest saw he had ever seen. The moonlight shining into his bedroom reflected onto his face from the surface. Victoria looked Liam straight into his eyes, no more than two inches away from his and spoke. "Think you are better than me now do you? Goodbye" as the saw severed the tops layers of skin with its first stroke. Liam was still hoping that this was some disgustingly awful vivid nightmare and in any moment he would wake up in a cold sweat. He never of course, he just continued to see the saw fall deeper into his waist band until death caught up to him.

Victoria stood over the body of the now ex magician and marvelled that the ideas she had thought about had worked. However, all the time she had spent waiting for them to stop arguing and waiting for Liam to drink himself tired had given her another idea.

Five minutes it took her to draw an eye winking on his chest with her home made weapon. She was so pleased that it actually looked like what it was supposed to be, she signed 'Liam' onto his upper thigh too.

Hayley still lay sound asleep in the passenger side of the car as Victoria past it. As the car door shut behind her and she removed part of her kill suit, Victoria held a large stone in her hand. She started the engine and as she drove past, threw the stone at the car that Hayley was asleep in. This of course woke her up, she turned around to see the front door open so she went inside to investigate.

Chapter 9

"How could that jumped up little shit let Stephen out of his site? I mean how did he get out of the house without him seeing anything but walk back into it as brazen as you like?" Wallace ranted to Atkinson.

"How do I know? Unless he fell asleep which he isn't admitting to, I have no clue. Both exits from the front and back of the house lead to where he could have seen him leaving."

The conversation continued along these lines for another twelve minutes until they reached Liam and Hayley's house on Pickering Road. Atkinson got out of the car and immediately noticed the park and woodland area almost opposite their house. As they entered the house sans Hayley, who had been taken to the Police Station already, they could smell the stench of death in the air. The Detectives approached the Officer who had been waiting for them to arrive. He had made himself a cup of tea and some toast whilst he waited, after all forensics had been and gone by now as well as the arresting Officers who had taken Hayley into custody for suspected murder.

"So" the Officer started, rubbing the crumbs from around his mouth "I guess fellas you are here because of this" and held his arm out to guide them up the stairs. "If you ask me, I reckon it is some love interest's revenge killing."

"We didn't ask" Wallace snapped. "And we will make our minds up for ourselves" Atkinson butted in.

The pungent stench was becoming unbearable but nothing either of them hadn't come across before. As they turned onto the landing at the top of the stairs they could see Liam's feet at the end of his bed, and as they walked closer they saw where his lower torso ended and his upper torso began. they where totally separated from each other.

"So these two are some sort of magical act" the Officer began to inform them "they had been performing at the New Theatre last night and neighbours said that they heard very raised voices upon their return, with one stating that Mrs Rowbotham had left the house and sat in the car with a duvet and a pillow. Both of those items were indeed in the car when the Officers arrived."

"So why are we here?" Atkinson asked.

"Because of the nettles and the string. Someone obviously had to forethought to bring a string of stinging nettles tied together to, what it looks like, rub over his body before he was killed."

"What, stinging nettles?" Wallace asked with bemusement.

"Yes and the rope, which can be bought from joke or magic shops like the one in Hepworth's Arcade in town, was tied around his cock and bollocks, his sack was sliced, exposing his raw testicles, but they are missing."

"So?" Atkinson asked, becoming weary of this Officer by the second.

"Well according to Joyce in forensics, who is a massive fan of his, he has never used a string in any of his acts, nor nettles. His garden is also all covered in slate and no nettles are there either."

"But the wife could have got the nettles from the park across the road though" Wallace announced but stopped when he saw the etching that had been carved into Liam's chest with his name underneath. "It's him" Wallace said with quiet conviction in his voice to Atkinson "I bet you twenty".

"How can you be so sure?" Atkinson asked.

"I just have a feeling with the etching and like the Officer said, the forethought with the nettles. Even if his wife had returned into the house, I doubt she would have ran across the road to the park, neatly tie up some nettles and rub them over his body before killing him. The string didn't convince me but I just know it is him."

"If you are right, then it could be that this Stephen is more dangerous than we initially thought. We're sure it's him aren't we? I am."

"If this and the other killings aren't his work, then he is up to something else that we don't know about."

The Officer left them to walk around the bedroom. They both took it in turns to stand in various parts of the bedroom and just look around them. Eight minutes past until Atkinson spoke up.

"If it wasn't the wife, the killer would have already had to be in here or walk past her in the car to get into the house. Surely you would hear someone walking on the shale, past the car if you were in it."

"Exactly, I just think that this looked all too prepared for the wife but I have been wrong lots of times before."

On their way back to the station there was no conversation between the two. If the radio hadn't have been bleating orders to his colleagues I swear they would have been able to hear each others cogs turning in their brains, trying out all scenarios possible in the minds.

Both men got out of the car, Wallace locked the car behind him with his key fob, greeted the Officer at the door with their badges, walked up into the crime room, picked up their telephones and called their boss. Within four minutes they were stood outside of the room where Hayley was being held. The arresting Officers did not look best pleased to see them, although they parted like school children when teachers turn up to break up a playground fight, as they all knew why they were there.

Atkinson and Wallace entered the room where Hayley was sat, make up still smeared down her face like a freshly painted doll in the rain and sat on one of their most uncomfortable chairs that they had in the station. It was saved for the most deserving people and brought out of a scrap room for occasions just like these.

The Detectives listened for thirty five minutes to Hayley's story, exactly how it had happened up until ringing the Police herself. She was protesting why she was a suspect when she had called it in but as it was explained to her, this happens a lot more than she thought. As the conversation continued, Wallace started to believe her story more and more. She stopped talking twice to retch into an already vomit lined bin that had been emptied twice for her.

"I just can't get the image out of my head" Hayley kept saying "Handcuffed, cut in half, a drawing carved into his chest, his genitals mutilated and nettles all over him."

"Do you recognise the symbol on his chest?" Wallace asked.

"No, to be honest I never really had a good look at it as I was too distraught. What is it?"

"To us it looks like an eye winking on his chest and his name carved onto his thigh" Atkinson explained.

Hayley hands raised up to her mouth in astonishment, both Detectives watched as the obviousness that she knew something about it was clear for even the weakest of psychics to pick up on it.

"What does that mean to you?" Wallace asked.

"Last night when we came out of the stage door, Liam signed a women's thigh at her request and he winked at her as he stood up so I let her boyfriend feel my arse whilst having his picture taken with me. That is what we were arguing about when we came home."

The Detectives looked at each other, halted the interview, stepped out of the interview room and told the Officers to replace Hayley's chair with a more comfortable one. As they sat in the adjacent room, they surmised that the killer must have either already been in the house or seen this happen outside of the stage door. He could even have been the boyfriend of the girl who had her thigh signed. Wallace turned around and told the gawking Officers to pull their thumbs out of their arses, look on social media for these two and get them in for questioning.

Atkinson however still thought that it could be Hayley and that they could end up chasing a dead lead when the killer was already arrested. "Why don't we just keep her here until we know for definite? We have enough evidence to do so and if we are wrong, we apologise and release her." Wallace agreed, just in case his partner was correct but wanted to be at the post mortem to see what Joyce had to say. She wasn't the most professional of forensic scientists that Wallace had met but her reports where the most detailed he had ever seen. If he had ever needed anyone to be in court with him on a difficult case, she would be the person to have on his side.

Later in the day the two Detectives stood covered in a blue apron and gloves, in the presence of Joyce Parker. She had 'amusingly' placed Liam's feet touching his head on the slab so both severed ends were facing the outside of the table.

"This person was good at his shit" she announced "I have been to see him quite a few times, I even got to shake his hand once. Now I can shake whatever I want I suppose" and snorted a laugh towards the Detectives, both of them staring at each other and face palming themselves. "No, not your cup of tea? What about the fact that he had a very small needle mark on the inside of his elbow? I have sent a tox screening off to see if anything was in his system before the time of death, I should have the results for you by the end of the evening unless something is found that isn't used regularly, then it should be the morning."

"This Joyce is why you are the best" Wallace told her. She looked coy for a moment and replied with "Stop shit licking me Wallace, I don't need any praises, and I know how good I am. Besides it can't have been anything to make his cock bigger, I mean look at him, poor soul. No wonder he did magic, it was obviously some sort of compensation."

"I wasn't shit licking (doing the speech marks in mid air with his fingers gesture towards her), I was telling you the truth."

"I've told you before, you can't have any of this" rising her hands up from her thighs to her chest with her fingertips, covering her whole body "I already have a fine collection that would put both of you to shame, and especially poor Liam here" and she winked.

She continued her work, speaking into a bluetooth headset the whole time. After seven minutes she paused and looked at both of them and asked "If you are waiting for the cause of death then you aren't as good as I thought you both were."

"No, we are just admiring your work" Atkinson piped up "We like watching you work."

"Pervs, leave me alone while I caress each part of his body with my tongue in peace" and gave them both a wicked smile. The Detectives shook their head, turned around and left before they found out if she was being serious or not.

Both men left the room and returned to the office to check up on Stephen Wetherall's whereabouts for the dozenth time that day. According to the Officer watching he was still at work, doing overtime apparently. The detectives pleaded with the Officer to stay awake tonight which was met with ferocious denials and they laughed together. They kept their superior updated with what was happening and when they had finished their paperwork, they made their way to the car park.

Wallace pressed the fob key to unlock the car door and they both opened their corresponding doors. The sight of the unsheathed testicles on their dashboard made both of them jump simultaneously.

Chapter 10

Victoria was extremely pleased with herself at getting the testicles inside of the right car just at the right time. She had watched at the ensuing melee as the Detectives leapt out of their car looking around the car park for the man watching them, she of course even though she was disguised, was not even considered to be the person who had left them. Instead she had exited the car park with ease, through the station and out of the front doors.

As it was time for her shift to start, she changed out of her wet clothes into her work uniform. Even though there were parking spaces outside of the shop, Martin wouldn't allow her to park there as that was for the convenience of their customers. Instead she had to park a few minutes away on Brooklands Road, which was far enough to get soaked through her coat into her clothes. Thank fully she had enough forethought to bring her work clothes in a separate bag to get changed into when she got there. There was no staff changing rooms and she knew that in the back room Martin would be stood, trying to peek a glimpse at her body. She didn't mind, he was alone and it was her fault so she would allow him a glimpse of her nakedness now and again. His last girlfriend had become increasingly jealous of their working relationship which had caused them to break up. Victoria had felt sorry for him as he was a genuinely nice man and deserved someone to share his life with.

As soon as she walked into the shop there was a couple looking around as well as another couple already with Martin, sat at his desk talking shop. She didn't believe in the hard sell approach so she introduced herself to the second couple and told them that she was available if they needed her. Only a few minutes past when the woman walked up to Victoria and asked her about the different styles of bedroom furniture that they offered. Of course as usual, she recommended her favourite style and the one where she was able to view them as easy as possible for a few weeks before finally making the decision to rid the word of them.

"We have this contemporary style with an open plan which is unusual but definitely in at the moment. Plus it saves you money as you aren't paying for the doors, the frames of the fitted furniture are stronger than the usual materials used in the more typical furniture that is more common in most people's homes."

Victoria made sure that she emphasised the words 'typical' and 'common' in her spiel to entice them into buying the set she wanted. This couple however wanted the more common style of bedroom which immediately turned off the switch inside of her head that would memorise their bedroom size and layout of the room for future personal use.

She couldn't convince everybody that came into the shop but enough for her to gradually feed her need to kill those who were less important to the cause than her. The bedroom turned out just how the couple had imagined and because they had snubbed her suggestion of bedroom furniture, she ensured that they spent the maximum amount that they could afford without pushing them too much to leave without buying it from them. There was nothing she liked less than customers spending all that time going through the plans, developing the plans and them walking away to 'think it over'.

Both couples left happy but Victoria was empty. She obviously had a back log of couples who had previously bought the bedroom she had recommended, but she was still keen to get as many as she could if for any reason the shop closed. There were other ways she could watch people if the bedroom situation changed but she was a creature of habit and now she had the bedroom set up down to an art form.

When she got home, the folder full of past customers who had chosen her bedroom was retrieved from its hiding place and the paperwork was strewn across the front room floor. When she began using this method of choosing her next victims, she had used the 'eeney meeny miney mo' way of deciding who was next. Now however, she looked into every intricate detail to ensure that she predicted almost every scenario in case she had to ad lib any of her routine.

Six bedrooms later, Victoria finally picked her next victims but read the rest of them in case she changed her mind. That almost happened but she put them on top of the pile for next time instead.

Wasting no time she suited up and drove close to the house she was about to go inside. She looked around for the best vantage point from outside the front of the house without being noticed, which she found.

There was a collection of overgrown bushes that she could get an incredible vantage point from. Plus this house was easier to watch as it had a school behind the house. She could stand on the grounds and look onto the back of the house without ever being seen. The fence at the back of the house separating the school from their back garden was both flimsy and easy to get through for someone of Victoria's stature.

Once she had watched from the front and back of the house for a week each, she easily penetrated the fence and into the rear of the Jenkins' property. Staring up at the back bedroom window, left slightly ajar because of the heat was easily enough for her to take advantage of.

The inside of the house was nice and warm with nobody occupying the aforementioned bedroom. People really did make it easy for her to invite herself into their homes. Other homes she had got into had their doors unlocked, windows open and no alarms. She was thankful of this of course otherwise it would make her life a lot more difficult.

As she silently sneaked onto the landing of the house, she looked at the other three doors facing her. In her mind one belonged to a bathroom and the other two were either bedrooms or one room used as something else. The sounds of the snoring led her to the room she really wanted to be in, easing the door open she saw the couple curled up facing each other fast asleep. On the way into the room, she looked to her left and saw the furniture were she would be spending the next couple of weeks watching them to pick up any routines. It was perfect and as it should be, just as she had explained to them when she was selling them it. They hadn't rested anything in front of the open plan setting, placed the clothes exactly had she had recommended and even left her enough room to get in comfortably.

As she left the property the same way that she had entered it, she smiled to herself that she was that good at what was important to her. She got back into her car, returned home and masturbated furiously until she fell asleep.

Early the next morning Victoria was again inside of Jenkins' house again; this time making herself aware of any loose floor boards, squeaks and other things that could make a noise to compromise her work. After ninety minutes of meticulous investigation, she was happy with the fact that she could move anywhere in the house without making a single sound. Next came the viewings at night to perfect her practice and think about how best to rid them from her world. The use of the pancuronium bromide has been a success so she planned on using it again on both of them.

Over the next two weeks listening to their bedtime routine and watching them as they came to bed and how they slept she was knew that the next night would be perfect. Victoria shuddered with delight at the thought of twenty four hours from now.

Chapter 11

The Jenkins had been in their house since 4pm and Victoria had been there before them. She had to get there earlier than usual, but seeing as though she had chosen a Sunday, it had been possible. The clinking of the cutlery from downstairs at dinner time and the smell of the cooked roast made her saliva glands drip into overtime. The smell of the Yorkshire puddings in the oven and roasting meat brought back memories from when Victoria's mother used to make them sit down in the front room and watch TV, whilst she worked her fingers to the bone to produce a culinary masterpiece.

Her mother was dearly missed by her whole family, she had been taken from this world far too early. The kitchen was her mother's space and no-one dare enter it in fear of receiving smaller helpings or none at all. She died when she was forty one, caused from a pulmonary embolism from an unknown source. It had taken Victoria an extraordinary amount of time to grieve enough for her to become social again. At the wake she recalled members of her family stating that you could not second guess God's work. At first Victoria had felt herself raging at this statement but also remembered what thoughts she had and felt her teeth biting the inside of her lip to refrain her from spurting out a hypocritical tirade. She knew that there was some sort of higher being pushing her along the path of her inner most thoughts and when she was brave, clued up and intelligent enough she would undertake what she was meant to do.

The bed springs depressing on the Jenkins new mattress signalled the time for Victoria to cease reminiscing and to take charge of the matter in hand. The woman liked to keep her bed side light on so she could read, whereas the man would usually mess about on his phone before falling into a deep slumber. The wife would, more often than not turn his phone onto standby and continue to read until the tiredness beat her too. Tonight however, from Victoria's vantage point, both had drifted off at about the same time. This would change things but only slightly, as she clambered out from her hiding place and looked at the couple fast asleep in the semi lit room.

The curtains of the room were closed as she had heard from her previous nights watching, that Mrs Jenkins (Amanda) thought that one of their neighbours used to watch her undressing when the curtains were open. This amused Mr Jenkins (Rob) as he knew that the person whom she was referring to probably had little else in his life than his petty voyeurism of his neighbours. He had agreed to close the curtains though only to appease his self-conscious wife.

They looked so helpless and innocent as he lay on his back with his phone on his stomach, still half resting in his right hand and her with her book lying next to her; her too on her back. The bag was pulled out from under the bed and carefully opened. The needles were laid side by side and prepared for the inevitable as Victoria scaled the bed from the foot end. She crouched on all fours being careful not to waste any of the pancuronium and soil the scene, otherwise it would be easier to trace. Her crawling was so slow and precise that it hardly made the bed move, the loaded needles rose above her head and with almost complete synchronicity, they were jabbed into each person's stomachs. Rob's body flung into action for the few seconds it allowed him to until the chemical took hold of him, leaving his body laid on his front making the needle snap inside of his torso. Amanda however could not have felt a thing as she remained still after the penetration.

Victoria did not like this, so began to slap her a few times to bring her around, when that did not work she nipped Amanda underneath her left upper arm and inner right thigh. After there was still no response so she felt for her pulse and there wasn't one. Either by sheer coincidence she had passed away in her sleep before Victoria could kill her, or she had used too much pancuronium and had overdosed her immediately.

Out of absolute frustration she kicked Rob's body back over onto his back, his eyes pierced hers for the first time since they had met at the shop, even though he did not know who she was as she was protected by her kill suit. The original idea to do the same to Rob as she had done to Liam went out of the window, she would make him pay for his wife's weakness and finish with the same.

As Victoria took hold of Rob's mass of curly hair, she pulled his head forward so his chin almost touched the top of his chest. "You are going to pay more for the inadequacies of your late wife" and tears began to trickle down the side of his cheeks. "I see you are just as weak as she is, good job that your existence won't be bothering me for much longer".

The pliers came out of the bag and Rob's eyes widened, she began to tease him which part of his body was going to be chosen. She hovered them about his fingers, then his toes, moving up to pyjama bottoms to his groin. The pliers pressed against his genitals but waved her finger in the air from side to side as if to show him that it would be them. The pliers eventually moved up his body and without notice grabbed his left nipple between its jagged teeth and twisted them around.

On the fourth twist Rob's skin began to break, allowing Victoria to peel it and some of the surrounding flesh away from his body. As the nerve endings from the wound dangled in front of Rob's face, she dropped it onto his chest and began twisting right one. This nipple was less tough than the last to free from his torso and she dangled that in front of his face before dropping it next to the other one.

Victoria leant over to see where the bag was and dropped the pliers into it. She sat astride of Rob and turned her head from side to side, maintaining eye contact with him and playing about with his torn nipples on his chest as if she were sensually teasing him. From nowhere she produced her unique weapon, leant back and slashed the inside of Rob's legs, severing both of his femoral arteries. As she watched the blood ooze out of the wounds, she grabbed in between his legs and felt around for two presents that she would leave for the Detectives again. After all, they had been so surprised the first time, why not surprise them again. She sliced open Rob's scrotum and carefully removed his testicles, once she had them in her hand she looked up to see that his chest was no longer moving and on closer inspection his pulse had ceased too. The testicles were placed in a bag and sealed it using the plastic zipper at the top.

Upon exiting the house and walking down the street, she became aware of someone watching her but as she turned around she could not see anyone. She did not have time to stand in the middle of the lit road staring at all of the bedroom windows, so she got into her car further down the road and started the engine, her eyes darting to each side of the road to look out for anybody attempting to her from her. She saw no-one.

Once she had disappeared the person stepped out from behind a parked van and walked in the opposite direction that Victoria went.

Chapter 12

Joyce Parker stood in the middle of the car park holding up Liam's testicles in two sets of chopsticks. "Sautéed or par boiled?" she announced to all of the onlookers.

"For fucks sake Joyce, bag em up" Wallace ordered.

"You lot are no fun sometimes, if you'd have waited I would have hidden them for you and you could have probed me anywhere to find them" winking at him and licking her lips. Atkinson saw this and interrupted quickly.

"Do you think they are Mr Rowbotham's?"

"Would you like me to suck them and check if they taste the same as the inside of his scrotum?" and looked at him like he was the crazy one.

"No need to be sarky Joyce, just get it done" and Atkinson walked towards Wallace who had skulked away following Joyce's proposal towards the car.

"I can't help wondering how he got in here, in the car and left without anyone noticing anything or catching anyone suspicious on the cameras" Wallace announced. "I don't know Wallace, if I did we would be chasing him down right now" Atkinson replied, "Check on Stephen Wetherall, see if he has left or not left and returned again." The moment Wallace retrieved his phone from his pocket when it rang. "Yes?"

"You are not going to believe this but Stephen went out so one of us followed him, but I stayed at the house" the Officer informed him.

"And?"

"He has just left the house again with no sight of either him returning or my partner, so I have decided to follow him."

"I see, have you tried to contact your partner?"

"Yes and he hasn't answered. I am just on Holderness Road near East Park now and he is heading towards Woodford."

"Keep following him and I will get dispatch to keep trying him okay and we will get there as soon as we can" and hung up. He signalled to Atkinson to get into the car and they set off as quick as they could.

As they got onto Holderness Road they called the Officer again "Where are you?" Atkinson asked. "Following Stephen back down Laburnum Avenue, he walked up to Woodford, looked around and now he's on his way home."

"Stop walking, NOW!" and he did. "I have done, why?"

"He knows you are following him that's why? Now turn around and walk back onto Holderness Road" and as he did his jaw hit the floor "What the fuck?" the Officer said and the phone hung up.

When Atkinson told Wallace what had happened he put his foot down and sped down Holderness Road and too fast down Laburnum Avenue until they saw three men near Stephen's house. As they drove closer, now slowing down, they saw the Officer who had been on the phone, with Stephen in the middle and the Officer's partner on the other side of Stephen. They exited the car and walked up to the three men.

"Good evening Stephen, how are you doing?" Wallace asked.

"Well I was doing okay until these two stopped me in the street and made me stay here until you two arrived, what do you want?"

"We want to know how you can leave the house twice, without returning to it" Atkinson asked.

"What ARE you talking about, I haven't left the house twice."

"No he hasn't" the Officer's partner piped up which made Stephen double take.

"What do you mean, no he hasn't? How do you know?" and after a couple of seconds the penny dropped. "Have you been following me?" and the Officer's partner did not respond.

"You are aren't you? Why?" Stephen asked again, now more demanding.

"You are the only person who we interviewed that doesn't have an alibi for a case we are investigating and you tick certain boxes which gives us cause for concern." Wallace informed him.

"I never knew that couple, I already told ya!" becoming more agitated now.

"Calm down" Atkinson told him.

"Why should I? I haven't done anything to anyone and yet you think I am capable of killing someone. I'm a furniture fitter."

"So how have you managed to slip past our men twice leaving the house but not being seen?" Atkinson asked.

"He hasn't" the Officer's partner stated again.

"What do you mean he hasn't?" Atkinson enquired.

"I have been behind him since he left the house, I never lost him once." Atkinson turned to Stephen was a quizzical look "How are you doing it?" but Stephen kept quiet.

"Look if you explain what is going on here you will absolve yourself in the case we are looking into and you will be able to stop wasting our time" Wallace stated but again Stephen remained silent. "Take him in" Wallace told the Officers, "we will question him more then." The Officer grabbed an arm each and informed him that he was being arrested for the possible murder of Mr and Mrs Duckerton and someone called Liam Rowbotham.

"Who is he?" Stephen asked.

"Oh, now all of a sudden you speak?" the Officer said with sarcasm laced his voice as he lowered Stephen's head into the back of the Detective's car.

"What do you think is going on?" Atkinson asked Wallace. "Well he is either a magician or..." and Wallace's head turned towards Stephen's house and began walking briskly towards it.

"Where are you going?" Atkinson questioned but when he got no answer, he followed him instead and as Wallace got to the door he started banging on it.

"This is Detective Wallace Wallace, let me in. We have Stephen and if you want to stop him going to prison for killing three people that he didn't do, answer this bloody door."

"What are you thinking? There is no such thing as splitting yourself in two so there must be someone else in this house that he doesn't want us to see." He banged on the door again but louder "Come to this door or I will ring my boss so I can smash it down, either way I am getting in."

When he didn't get an answer, Wallace got out his mobile phone and began to ring the boss. As he said hello he heard the locks clicking on the other side of the door.

The door opened and there stood Stephen Netherall.

Chapter 13

"What the fuck is going on?" Wallace shouted; looking at Stephen stood in the doorway and looking back at their car, but Stephen in the doorway remained silent. "Oh I am getting sick and fucking tired of this silent treatment" Atkinson said, shouting too "Get him in your car and take him to the station" he told the Officers.

As both cars pulled into the station car park neither Stephen had said a word for the whole journey, even though Wallace and Atkinson had tried their best for the first Stephen to say something; anything to shed some light on this situation. Atkinson got onto the radio and told the Officer to take the second Stephen in first and put him in a room for away from their usual one. All three of them watched as the two officers and the second Stephen walked out of the car park, through a fire door and disappearing inside. They gave them a few minutes for him to be booked in and they left their car with the first Stephen and took him to an interview room on a different floor.

All four men walked into Chief Inspector Wallis' room and explained their situation.

"Tell me that you have some evidence from their house that can put either of them in the Duckerton's or the Rowbotham's house?" Wallis asked hopingly.

"Forensics are in there now, we just have to wait" Atkinson announced.

"So you burst into their home uninvited and sent a forensic team inside without their permission?" Wallis stated.

"No Sir" Wallace began "One of them opened their door and when we asked if we could go inside or send a team inside, neither of them refused us entry."

"Oh good, so did they tell you anything?"

"No Sir, they are both keeping their mouths shut which is both highly annoying and suspicious" Atkinson answered for them all. Wallis looked at the two Officers and dismissed them from the room, thanking them for their assistance in this matter.

"I want one of you to look into all incomings and outgoings to that house, the other one of you has to go and see Joyce while I go and see them both myself."

"I'll do the searching" Atkinson answered as quick as venom entering an unsuspecting victim, he looked at Wallace who was staring daggers from his eyes in Atkinson's direction. "Thanks" was his only response.

Wallace walked into the Pathology department and as he walked through the second set of doors, before Joyce could have seen him, she shouted "Now then gorgeous, if you came to see me working with the testicles you are far too late"

"How did you know it was me?"

"I can smell you from the lift, I have terrific sense of smell and hearing. Now come over here and look at my statistics, that's why you came right? So to speak" nudging him on the left arm and winking. They both walked towards her desk and sat down.

"There was a chemical in Mr Rowbotham's body that contributed to his death but it was different to the one found in Mr Duckerton or the one placed on his wife. Are we sure that this is the same killer's handy work? The previous kills have all used the same anaesthetic that was used on the Duckertons."

"I am positive Joyce. I think he is becoming more comfortable and full of his own self-importance that he is trying new techniques, but the kills are far too similar."

"So have you got your guy?" she asked becoming more professional, flicking over from humour like a light switch. "*Guys*" he replied "Identical twins."

"That could be why some of the murders are ever so slightly different then."

"Maybe Joyce, maybe. I'd better go back and see if the boss has made any leeway with either of them."

Wallace stood up walked over to the first set of double doors, turned around and saw that Joyce had been watching every step that he had made. She waved at him by twinkling each one of her fingers at him very slowly and seductively, then spinning her hand around to flip him the middle finger salute. She turned around like nothing had happened, back to her computer screen.

As Wallace exited the lift, he saw his Wallis walking towards him with a big smirk on his face and before he could ask him why, he told him.

"You need to check in with Atkinson and if what they said is right, you could be making a very grovelling apology" walking straight past him and into his office. "Why?" but he didn't get a response, again. He was coming extremely pissed off at people not talking to him today.

Atkinson was on the telephone and welcomed Wallace into the room with a wave telling him to hurry up and listen into the conversation that he was having. As Wallace approached he could hear the other person on the end of the phone "....and I can only apologise for the actions of my sons Detective" the woman on the other line said. "Okay, Mrs Netherall I will see you in a couple of hours." After they had both bid each other farewell and ended the call, Atkinson turned towards Wallace and gave him a rather large embarrassed smile. "Well?" Wallace asked.

"You heard the end of it right?"

"Yes but I don't know anything before since we left the bosses office until now."

Atkinson told Wallace the whole story of how both brothers acted as one so they could cheat Nobel & Sons into paying them for work that both of them had done. Stephen's twin brother Roger had been fired for having a steamy affair with Mr Nobel's daughter but had agreed to keep Stephen in a job.

Since then both brothers had been living in the same house but only one of them going to work at any, making it look like Stephen was working from early morning to the last thing at night. The only other person who knew what was going on was their mother who was quite happy to go along with it as long as they were both making money and Roger could still claim job seekers benefit. That was the main reason that both of them would not speak to the Detectives at first because they thought that owning up would land them in jail. However, after speaking to Wallis for five minutes each, the possibility of being charged for murder instead of something less trivial such as benefit fraud soon got them spilling the beans.

"So we are at square one again?" Wallace sighed.

"It certainly seems that way yes"

The only other person at the furniture warehouse that they had a small suspicion about was no longer in the picture either as he had come up with a credible alibi which had been investigated and found to be true. Both men sat on the shared desk with their hands cupping their chins, feeling sorry for themselves that again they had nothing.

All leads led to a dead end again until the bodies of Rob and Amanda Jenkins were found.

Chapter 14

A "Can you help these two please Victoria?" from Martin was the reason this couple were about to be the next victims. If he had just taken the time to serve them himself, they would still be enjoying their new bedroom for years to come.

"Yes of course" and sat down at her desk. "Hi there, I'm Victoria, how can I help you?"

"Well" Jan answered "We are looking for a complete refit of our bedroom whilst we can still afford to do it."

Jan and her husband Tim were both in the mid-fifties and besides visiting their family in Turkey, they wanted to make sure that their house was all set up for when they decided to retire. They didn't want to get to retirement with any room not refurbished or in a state of ill repair. I mean, how many years of your retirement do you actually see? Some people see a couple of decades whilst others are not so fortunate.

"Well if you tell me your expected price range and I will tell you exactly what you can have for that amount" and the couple looked at each other for a few seconds and nodded. The amount of time that they had been together, both of them knew what that look meant.

"Our top level amount is two thousand five hundred, is that okay?" Jan replied.

"That's fine, now let's see what we can get you for that."

Unfortunately Jan and Tim, even though they did not have that much to spend, stuck to their guns when Victoria had tried selling them the wardrobes that she liked the best. She was about to give up on even ever seeing them again when Jan piped up. "Is there any way we can have a deeper bed for more storage but keep in our price range?" and it made Victoria smile inwardly. She would have to change her routine but if she made it possible to be able to hide under there, it was totally doable.

"So what do you do?" Victoria asked them during one of the lulls in the conversation when they were waiting for the computer to refresh.

"I'm a bus driver" Tim replied, "and I am a cleaner" said Jan.

"Interesting" Victoria quipped and immediately, just as she had wanted, the couple told them other jobs they had done. "I used to work at a chocolate factory in the city and he used to be a butcher" trying to make up and improve her standing after Victoria's jibe. Now those jobs really did interest her. The transaction was completed and both the couple and Victoria ended that day full of inspiration and anticipation.

That was thirteen weeks and two days ago. Right now, Victoria was laid underneath Jan and Tim in one of the drawers that she had helped them choose. This place had been chosen to hide as soon as Jan had mentioned the extra room, and as soon as she was able to get inside of the house she had tried to fit herself inside of it. If she was unable to get into it, she would have either had to concede defeat or try something that she had never done before, and wait in another room.

She didn't feel that she was ready for that much distance between them and her, but it didn't matter in the end as she did fit. Once she knew that she could fit in it, she could now spend night after night under their bed without them knowing. How many times do people actually look under their beds? Most of the time it is children who do and these two where far from that stage in their lives. Once you stored something under there, you hardly ever look there again, unless you can't find something and then it all comes out.

She had been under this bed on twelve occasions and now she was more than confident that she could rid them quite easily with the smallest amount of energy expended. The next night would be the perfect time to rid the world of their existence.

Victoria had gone one step further with these two as she had made sure that she met them again by 'accident' before the kill. On more than one occasion Victoria had got onto

Tim's bus and made sure that he had made eye contact, whereas she had passed Jan on her bike on her journey to work on a few occasions too, making sure she knew who she was. This was a new and more outlandish step in the wider scheme of things and something she had enjoyed doing so much that she thought that she might want to meet them before the kill more often.

The outside of their house looked magnificent in the dimly lit evening, the front of it welcoming Victoria into its walls. She could hear the house reminding her which way was the easiest to enter and how she should move through the house, without turning any lights on but making sure that no-one knew that she had been there before them. She pulled out the drawer from underneath where Tim laid, emptied it and placed the contents in the drawer under where Jan slept and in the remainder of the room underneath the bed.

Once the drawer was empty she put her bag of tricks in the drawer first and got in after it. As soon as she was comfortable she pushed against the frame of the bed, making the drawer disappear underneath the bed and waited. If she was right; Jan would be the first one home in just under twenty minutes, followed by Tim about an hour later.

Sure enough not long after 6.30pm Jan approached on her push bike, she opened the back gate which was always left unlocked, left her bike next to the bin, unlocked the back door and left it unlocked behind her for Tim to get into the house later. She didn't know that the back door had already been unlocked and locked again behind Victoria whilst she finished preparing the evening meal she had begun in the morning. By the time Tim walked through the back door and had eaten his meal, Victoria was ready and prepared for the events of the night to unfold.

The sounds of them both laughing at the television penetrated the floor underneath Victoria and into the drawer where she was waiting and at ten o'clock as usual, the television was turned off and both of them walked up the stairs in silence. The sound of clothes being taken off, teeth being brushed and clothes being put back on again was followed by the weight of both of them laying onto the bed. With Tim taken care of the moment that his weight had landed on his side of the mattress as the needle had penetrated his behind and the plunger pressed within a second of him laying down. Jan turned over to him to wish him goodnight, only to find him already asleep. Victoria had used the anaesthetic she had originally used, the kind that put you to sleep before an operation.

The sound of Jan tutting could be heard clearly that Tim had fallen asleep and as she turned back so saw a blur next to her bed, not being able to see properly without her glasses on. Her gaze rose up and as she did the palm of Victoria's hand hit Jan in-between the eyes as hard as Jan had ever felt in her life. The dizziness caused was short as Jan had been knocked out temporarily. This gave Victoria enough time to return to Tim, guide her weapon down his chest slowly inserting it deeper into his body the closer it got to his navel. When the weapon had become deep enough into Tim stomach, Victoria reached into the wound and grabbed hold of the nearest thing she could find and she pulled. Once she had emptied the wound of everything she had found, Victoria slapped Jan on her face until she awoke. When she saw Tim in the state of disembowelment, the screams were muffled by the makeshift gag from a pillowcase, her eyes wide open from the sheer violence that had unfolded next to her.

"He should count himself lucky because he didn't feel a thing" Victoria explained. "However, you are going to be able to feel every slice, poke and tear as I make it" and pierced Jan's skin with the needle with pancuronium in it. She had made sure that she had the correct amount in this time, not to overdose her like she had Amanda Jenkins.

As the weapon lacerated Jan's skin on her stomach, Victoria observed her facial expressions and her eyes to determine how much pain she was actually in but unable to express verbally or physically. The satisfaction of this only made her carry on even slower as she slid three fingers inside of Jan's now open wound and then followed by her thumb. She grabbed hold of Jan's intestine, not knowing if it was the smaller or larger and pulled. As her bowels left her body, she began to shake uncontrollably for about sixty seconds followed by nothing. Victoria felt for a pulse and it was still there, weak but still evident.

Victoria took solace in the fact that Jan would probably wake up eventually so she had to finish the job now and quickly. She lifted her bag onto the bed and unrolled a string of butchers knifes that she had found in their garage. They had been Tim's and he had proudly kept them in pristine condition since he had finished that stage of his career. Victoria grabbed hold of the cleaver and cut off one of Jan's feet, then plunged four of the knives into her chest. Next came the knife sharpener which Victoria grabbed, stood above Tim and drove it into his heart as deep as she could bury it, finishing it off with a three hundred and sixty degree twist just to make sure.

The remainder of the knives were packed into her bag of tricks and she left the house with the satisfaction that she could now fulfill her duties in two different ways.

As she disappeared into the night, the figure stepped out from the shadows and walked in the opposite direction.

Chapter 15

"This one has no bollocks either" Joyce told the two detectives as they walked through the door of the Jenkins' bedroom. Wallace's eyes rolled back in disbelief and she noticed.

"What's up sugarplum, don't you like me talking about genitals in front of your partner? You didn't seem to mind when we were alone." This made Atkinson turn around and look quizzically at Wallace, who shrugged his shoulders in bemusement and denying what she had said.

"Don't deny it because he is here" pointing at Atkinson with a piece of limp colon in her hand. "You know that you loved our special time together, now can we get back to work please?"

"We would love to Joyce if you could shut up for a minute" Atkinson told her.

"You're only jealous cos I didn't choose you and your sexy arse."

Atkinson's body hunched over as to ignore the compliment and walked over to Amanda's body, pushing past her as he did. Joyce looked over Atkinson's head as he past, gave a sultry look towards Wallace and pointed down almost touching Atkinson's head as she did. Wallace could not help but snigger but turned it into a cough when Atkinson looked up at him.

"So why do we think these are linked to our cases?" Wallace asked, trying to redeem himself in front of his partner.

"The killer used the same needles and from what I can gather so far; the same chemical as one of the other kills, they were obviously killed in their bedroom and this man's bollo....testicles have been removed just like the last one." Joyce answered assertively.

"But the woman hasn't been lacerated like the others, why?" Atkinson asked. Joyce put the three middle fingers of both hands and each side of her temple and began to hum loudly. After the ten seconds of humming halted, her hands dropped down by her sides, she turned her head to Atkinson and told him "Sorry, but my psychic ability is waning at the moment. Could you ask me again when my ether is more receiving."

"For fucks sake Joyce, can you be serious for a minute?"

"You stop asking me stupid questions, give me some time and I will stop fucking about. Just take it from me with all of my experience that I think this is the same killer. Now go out, do your job and catch this fucker so I can sleep at night without having to use my dildos as traps to catch someone sneaking in my house." She turned her attention back to Rob's body and shooed them out of the room with her left hand.

"Ring us when you know more please Joyce" Wallace asked, then both men did as they were told and left.

Atkinson was raging when he got back into the car and the steering wheel took the brunt of it all.

"I don't know why you let her get to you"

"It's not her, it's this fucking killer. How can he be so brutal but not leave a single clue? How can he have the forethought for every single scenario that could occur and still get it done without a single thing going wrong?"

"It has been a long year Nick I agree but we have to keep looking. The Officer said that the furniture came from the same place so I say we go back to the warehouse and the shop again. I am sure the answer is somewhere there."

Atkinson slumped over the dashboard, nodded his head and turned the key in the ignition. "I just know that his testicles are gonna turn up soon too".

"Lets start off at the Nobels and then go back to the shop" Wallace replied.

They arrived at Nobel and Sons seventeen minutes later. The vans were all parked up in the courtyard so Atkinson decided to park right in front of the entrance. They both got out of the car, Atkinson slamming his door still raging inside and swung open the front door of the warehouse. Inside Mr Walter Nobel and his son William were stood in front of his work force. They stood and listened to what was being said. Mr Nobel was warning any of his team of men and women that if they try to falsify their time sheets or try to pull the wool over his eyes they would be fired on the spot, just like the Wetherall brothers have been. As Walter finished his sentence he caught the two Detectives out of his peripheral vision and turned to look straight at them.

"How can we help you two?" Walter asked, inviting them to walk in front of his team. The Detectives stood in front of the people they had interviewed once before and looked out into the crowd. Wallace cleared his throat and began.

"We have spoken to all of you before about a previous case, well now we need to speak to you all again."

"Hang on" Walter interrupted "I lost enough money the first time from you two interviewing them all, you can't do it all again."

"We can and we will. I would like to do it now and use your office please."

Walter invited them into his office but Wallace stayed outside to make sure no-one left. Walter asked whether each person could get straight to work right after the interview and Atkinson agreed, so did he. Atkinson called Wallis and asked for a couple of Officers to stand guard outside so no-one escaped the warehouse.

It took four hours to interview everyone, explaining to each of them that matters discussed must not be shared with anyone else, no loved ones, other workers, the media and by no means mentioned on social media. Each one of the workers had again strong alibis which their team began investigating as soon as they called it in after speaking to each of them.

The Detectives thanked Walter for allowing them to eat into his day again and possibly lose money but they assured him that they would not have done it if it was not important enough. Walter was quite happy to allow them to look through his files of past employees too in case anything stood out to them. Time was getting on and they had to get to the bedroom shop so they made their excuses and left.

Wallace updated Wallis and made sure he directed their team into checking out the alibis of the Nobel's team. They explained that they were going to pay another visit to the shop then call it a day if they didn't find anything there, which they didn't expect to. Atkinson walked up gingerly to the car, fully expecting there to be another set of testicles in there, checking the dashboard before opening the door. Both men got inside and made their way to the shop.

Martin welcomed the Detectives into the shop just as he was about to lock up.

"Can I help you both? How's the investigation going" he asked.

"We can't discuss that but can we come in to talk to you again?"

"Well it is 5 o'clock and I am just about to go home" he looked at their faces, bedraggled and tiresome "but I suppose that I could spare a few minutes" and opened the door, welcoming them into the shop. The three men sat in the back of the shop, the Detectives with their arms on their knees and Martin, slightly fidgeting on his computer chair.

"Is there anyone else that you work with when choosing these bedrooms that you didn't tell us about the first time we came?" Wallace asked.

"No the only people responsible are us, the customers and the Nobels. Why is the investigation not going too well?" not meaning to sound patronising but did.

"We are just following up leads, were passing and thought that we would pay you a visit again."

"Doesn't sound like that to me fellas, it sounds like you are at a dead end and you are clutching at straws."

"We aren't at liberty to talk to you about our investigation and we just told you why we were here. Come to think of it, we didn't interview you last time did we?"

"Well you asked quite a few questions, yes" appearing more uncomfortable and the Detectives picked up on this.

"Where were you last night and can anyone back you up?"

"Well I was at home watching TV and no, I live alone." Atkinson and Wallace looked at each other, nodded and smiled.

"Would you join us down at the station please, we have some more questions to ask you?" Atkinson asked in his most smug yet polite voice.

"Am I under arrest?"

"No, we just want to eliminate you from our enquiries. You can come to Priory Police Station just up the road in your own car and meet us there if you like?" trying his best not to sound too cocky that they may finally have him. The minute they got in the car one of them would get a patrol car to follow him in case he tried to escape.

"Oh really? Tonight? I have loads to do tonight and I was planning a night of watching Breaking Bad."

"Look, what's more important? You watching some programme about a criminal or the reputation of your business when people find out why you were brought in for questioning?" Martin thought about that, knew he was being played and resigned himself to the fact that he would be spending the night with these two.

Martin grabbed his keys and coat, turned off the shop lights, closed the door behind him and let the shutters down whilst looking at two smug faces next to their car, parked right outside of the shop.

"My car is parked on Rosedale Grove over there. Do you want me to pull out of there and flash you when I am turning into the intersection so I can follow you?"

"Can do" Atkinson replied and they watched as he crossed the road and walked across the pelican crossing and down Rosedale Grove.

"Shall we get inside or wait for him to pull out of the road first?" Wallace asked.

"That's get inside in case he tries to make a break for it. You call in a patrol car." Atkinson ordered and both men opened their doors, Atkinson again checking the dashboard before he sat down.

Chapter 16

Victoria left work at 4.28pm, later than usual because she had made a very big sale for the company and the opportunity of watching the couple in the massive bedroom that they wanted furnishing made her tingle ever so slightly.

Her first visit would be to the local cheap shop to pick up some bargains. The shop used to be a big supermarket but since it has to close down due to bankruptcy, a man had taken it over and sold what can only be described as food past its best before date. He would more than likely get this food by the pallet load for next to nothing, from big companies then sell it in his makeshift supermarket. The food was perfectly fine for consumption but the big companies weren't allowed to sell it. The shop suited Victoria down to the ground as she didn't really like to spend that much money on food anyway. As long as it was nutritious, contained enough calories that would keep her going but not make her fat and kept her alive, she was fine with that.

Entering the shop she took her time to see that a new fridge had been installed and there was actually some fresh and short life foods on display today, although she didn't put any into her trolley. The whole of the inside of the shop was dark and dingy, not been decorated since the big name had moved out. Its high ceilings probably housed more fresh food than the new fridge did.

Victoria took her time walking around the shop and finally reached the till. There was only one person at the till and as she got closer she could hear the person talking to the owner.

"The stuff on the front of this tin looks worse than the bodies I look into every day" Joyce Parker was telling the man. "And this salami reminds me of an acquaintance that I should have kept in touch with." she continued, followed by a snort of laughter and a slight shove for the owner. Joyce moved down the bagging area and started placing her goods into the bags with a sultry look on her face, each item making her pull a more expressive pose as the next.

"Don't you just love putting things into bags?" she said in a smouldering mysterious voice, slightly turned around as she flayed her arms in an over dramatic pose, caught a glimpse of Victoria and stopped everything she was doing instantly. The rest of her shopping experience was performed in complete silence and she left the shop in silence too.

The owner looked at Victoria as she approached the till with her shopping.

"Thank god you turned up, I thought she was coming on to me that much that she would end up getting on her knees in front of me" and both of them gave a polite chuckle. The rest of the conversation between them was just exchanging money once she had finished packing her bags.

On exiting the shop she looked at her work place on the other side of the roundabout, and watched as the two Detectives walked into the shop and Martin closing it behind them. She knew what she had to do.

....

Atkinson patted his pockets as he sat down in the car. "Have you got the car keys?" he asked Wallace. "No you drove here, have you left them in the ignition?"

"It wouldn't surprise me" Atkinson answered and felt for the key. It was indeed still in the ignition. He turned it and fired the engine up. As his hand left the key he felt a strange sensation on the end of his fingers. He looked down, burst open the car door and leapt out. Wallace leapt out too but only because Atkinson had. He had no idea why he was doing so.

"FOR FUCKS SAKE!" Atkinson bellowed with his voice faltering in mid sentence.

"What is it? What the hells up with you?"

"There's a pair of fucking bollocks pierced onto the key chain of the fucking car keys" and Wallace found himself stifling his laughter as he knew Atkinson was furious.

"That's it" Atkinson started "I've had enough, I'm done with this case and this wacko." Wallace couldn't contain his laughter any more and guffawed into rapturous giggling.

"What the fuck are you laughing at?"

"I'm sorry, I know it's not funny but I can't help it" and Atkinson began to giggle.

"Why am I laughing now when I am shit scared?"

"Probably our bodies expressing it as laughter instead of going crazy. I will call it in, in a minute." and Martin pulled up beside of them.

"Are we off then?" he asked.

"No, you go home. We have more important things to do here. We will catch up with you soon though, okay?" Atkinson replied, just beginning to stop laughing. Martin looked puzzled and drove away slowly in case they were joking, they were laughing after all.

"You know what this means don't you?" Wallace asked his partner "Joyce will have to look at these." and the smile immediately wiped itself from Atkinson's face.

Victoria watched them from the other side of the roundabout at a bus stop, far away enough that they wouldn't notice her. At first she smirked at Atkinson's initial reaction but became angry when they both ended up laughing. How dare they laugh when she wanted to scare them? How dare they mock her accomplishments and the things that she had done? And how dare they think that Martin had anything to do with it? She would have to change what she was doing somehow, they were getting too close.

Chapter 17

"SHEEEEEE'S HEEEEEERE!" Wallace shouted, peeking his head out of the tent where the car was parked under. They had erected it when it had both started to torrentially down pour and the public were arriving in their droves.

Spring Bank West from Calvert Lane roundabout to the train bridge near Alliance Avenue had been closed off at rush hour so it wasn't the most popular move, hence people were coming to see what all the fuss was about.

Wallace was of course referring to Joyce Parker as she was allowed through the cordon of Police Officers stopping traffic passing.

"Well hello boys" she remarked to the Officers letting her through "I hope you are going to make it worth my while interrupting a seductive bath to come here" and watched as the young men squirmed with the thought. She got out of her Skoda Octavia and walked towards the tent, holding a magazine over her head. As she walked through the flaps of the tent, she threw the gay mens magazine at Atkinson. "I thought I'd get you this as you clearly like the feel of bollocks on your hand" she exclaimed and put on her protective uniform.

Atkinson stood emotionless, peeling the damp magazine from his face and upper chest area. He just pointed his finger at her and then to the inside of the car where the testicles were still dangling. Joyce walked over to the open car door and peered inside. She stood up straight and arched her back in fits full of laughter which continued for about twenty seconds.

"You have to hand it to this bloke, he definitely has a set of balls on him." Wallace and Atkinson looked at each other and literally put their palms to their faces.

"Well he has, to sneak into your car and have the time to pierce the testicles onto the keyring, that you'd left in the car I might add, then walk away like nothing has happened is both masterful and frightening."

"Masterful?" Wallace piped up looking slightly bemused.

"Yes masterful, how did he know where you where? Did he follow you around all day or just wait here to hope that you turned up? Come on, I'm not the Detectives around here, you are. Supposed to be anyways." and she saw Wallace hold onto Atkinson's coat to stop him from confronting her, followed by them leaving the tent. Joyce turned to one of her forensic colleagues and smiled.

"You know Gavin, twenty minutes ago I was only over there in that supermarket. I wonder if I sub consciously spotted him watching and waiting?" Gavin just shrugged his shoulders and carried on applying the coating for fingerprints.

In her mind, Joyce rewound the whole of her journey. From pulling up on Willerby Road just around the corner from the supermarket, visiting the local bakery for some home made Cornish pasties, into the newsagents for the gay mens magazine that she would be looking through later that night and walking across the pelican crossing, past the church, across another road and into the supermarket. She performed her journey back across the road, past the church and down Willerby Road to her stationary Skoda. To be honest, there had been quite a few dodgy characters on her journeys but all too obvious to be a psychotic serial killer, wasn't they? She would go through the mug shots back at the station once she has finished her, waiting for all the results to come back.

Joyce exited the tent with the forensic team, got out her phone and informed Wallis of how they got on. As expected, there had been numerous fingerprints in the car, they would have to eliminate all of them one by one which is always laborious. Plus she would see if the testicles did indeed match those of Rob Jenkins, which of course they did.

Victoria, who was still sat at the bus stop, saw the Skoda pull up and sat aghast as the loud, promiscuous woman from the supermarket got out of it, spoke to a couple of the Officers and entered the tent. When Atkinson and Wallace left the tent and got into their car she picked up the magazine she had purchased (one about celebrities and how skinny they all were) not because she liked it, it would be easy to hide behind if they were to pass the bus stop on the way around the roundabout. Another eighty two minutes past and Victoria stayed until she saw the woman leave with a small entourage, get back into her car and drive off herself. As Joyce's car went to pass, her phone rang. It was Martin.

She answered it and he explained everything that had gone on after she had left. The sympathetic reassurance she gave made him feel slightly better, although the scrumpy was doing the job too. He was scared that they suspected him for killing people in the bedrooms that had been purchased from his shop. He was a mess so Victoria agreed to go to his house to see him.

Twelve minutes later she was sat in his front lounge, drinking scrumpy with him.
"What am I going to do if this story gets out? We will both be out of a job and I will have to move and set myself up again far away."

"Stop panicking Martin, I am sure that is all just a huge coincidence that it is our bedrooms that these people are dying in. I mean come on, who would do that to us or the Nobels?"

"You never know what people are really like, I never do anyway" which Victoria was extremely grateful for, but she knew that the whole bedroom thing would have to be put on the back burner for now. She would have to find different and new ways of both ridding the planet of the less worthy but also keeping those Detectives chasing their tales and still knowing that it was her.

Laid down in bed that night, she thought. She thought for the next few weeks, trying to come up with an infallible way of achieving both scenarios, and it came to her.

Atkinson and Wallace sat in the crime room, almost a month after finding the testicles in the ignition and all of Joyce's work had come up with nothing substantial to point a finger at someone. There was a partial print on one of the keys but not enough to get a match from. The testicles were indeed Rob Jenkin's and they had even attended the couple's funeral in the background (as the did with each of the victims) in case the killer had decided to show up and they spotted him.

Wallis had called them into a meeting to re-evaluate their jobs and the case, he was pushing them harder than he ever had to try and come up with anything that would help to catch the perpetrator, but they all had ran out of ideas. Wallis knew that the usual time between kills was coming up so he decided to reluctantly get some help from a specialist from Liverpool. He was known world over for his ability to solve crimes that no-one else could. Wallis knew that the moment he requested him, it would probably be a few weeks until he arrived and his incessant ego trip would annoy the hell out of him, but something needed to be done. He may not even decide to come, he has done that before because he was too busy with other cases.

Atkinson and Wallace sat dejected as Wallis made the call; knowing that they had not done what they always dreamed of doing, being a Detective and cracking the largest case of their careers. They would now have to work with a man who, by his own words on his website, was "the best killer whisperer of his generation." They prayed that he was busy but a small part of them wanted his expertise to catch this bastard.

Joyce drove away from the crime scene outside the Bedroom shop and around the roundabout, she glanced over and spotted the woman who had been behind her in the queue at the supermarket.

She thought nothing of it and nor would she, until she met her again for the last time.

Chapter 18

It was the 3.36am and Michael was walking along the longest road on the journey from his night out clubbing to his house.

Boothferry Road was one of those roads were you are amongst houses and shops one minute, a dual carriage way and trees the next. He'd had a skin full as usual with his mates Carl, Wayne and Rod on a pub crawl. Then it had been time to frequent the local cess pool knocking shop of a nightclub.

There were a few to choose from but this particular night they had chosen the one were the theme was 'Grab a Granny night'. This meant that women from the age of 35 and over were basically up for anything from any man that approached them. It was a classy joint and it was well known city wide as well as the surrounding areas too.

Michael had been aware of a women he assumed was about mid to late thirties who had been eyeing him up since they had stepped through the door and began propping up the bar, at least thirty five minutes ago. Michael didn't mind the older lady, he always thought that the more the experience the better his night would be. Plus, most of these women were usually divorced or single parent mothers who all they wanted was their sexual needs met and no questions asked later. Funny really when decades ago it was all about the men going out looking for a good time to get away from their frumpy, nagging uninteresting wives. Now the shoe was on the other foot and all of a sudden the men were the prey instead of the predators.

Michael was twenty eight and had a string of failed relationships behind him, he thought this had been due to the women not appreciating his relationship with his tight group of friends. Whereas every single one of the women he had dated had been sick of the attitude he gave them whenever he had not gotten his own way on every single subject. He could be a really whingy whiny bastard when he wanted something and it didn't go his way. Sometimes to the point where he would literally stamp his feet on the floor as if to assert his authority.

The longest relationship he had managed was with Diane for three months and she had been extremely patient up to that point. The final straw was when he wanted to go to an air show with her but she had been unable to take the time off work so Michael had driven to Diane's workplace, walked into the manager's office and threatened him with violence unless Diane was granted the day off. The situation was resolved when Diane's boss had stood up from behind the desk, locked Micheal's arm behind his back, dragged him out of the workplace and slammed the door behind him. When Diane found out, she took her older brother with her and she dumped him like King Kong with an aeroplane.

Michael smiled back at the woman who took no time in standing up from the bar, walked around it staring at Michael for the duration and finally met him at the other side. She slid in between his friends like serpent fixed on its prey, took hold of his shirt and pulled him out from the group to their own space in the club. They stood there and small talked for about two minutes until he asked her to accompany him into the toilets. She agreed and it wasn't long before he was bending her over the toilet in the cubicle whilst she grabbed hold of the back of the cistern and was shagging the brains out of her. Three minutes later when he had finished, they were cleaning themselves up when she took a pen and a piece of paper out of her handbag and she gave it to him. Wrote on it was her phone number and address in case he wanted to do more of what they had just finished.

She left the cubicle and walked past the slightly geeky man who was stood at the urinal. He hid his penis in case she wanted to see it, she didn't and his urinating halted instantly. It only began again when he knew that she wasn't going to return. As soon as his urinating began again, Michael stepped out of the cubicle folding up the piece of paper into the top pocket of his shirt. He had a beaming smile across his face, that would do him tonight unless he was really lucky. He returned to his mates who wanted to know every single sordid detail. Fortunately three minutes of mediocre sex doesn't take too long to explain, so they were talking about the same old shit before they knew it.

Michael was the only lucky one that night as his other friends has spurned the attention of any willing females who even attempted to enter their space of bodily secretions. As usual they would all begin to walk home together until they reached each one of their houses one by one. Michael and Rod were the final two until Rod finally left him at Wheeler Street. This meant that Michael had another thirty minutes walk at least (depending on the path he chose to swerve) to his house.

As he walked under the underpass where trains barely pass over any more, he could see the first stretch of Boothferry Road in front of him. To his left there used to be the local football team's home ground, Boothferry Park, but now all that stood there were generic boring detached and semi detached houses will little or no character at all. He crossed the junction of North Road and the next five minutes would consist of houses and shops until he reached the next big roundabout with his old watering hole 'Fiveways'. This roundabout was affectionately known as Fiveways roundabout. It should have been called the hide about as people often thought that they were being watched as they walked adjacent to it, across the zebra crossings that surrounded it. You could not across the roundabout as it was full of bushes and trees. This is why people always thought that they were being watched.

As Michael crossed the second zebra crossing he could now see the seemingly endless road ahead of him. It would take him another twenty minutes at least to get home but it usually sobered him up. His mates were always jealous the next day when he would wake up fresh as a daisy whilst their mouths felt like an Inuit had bobbed there dead seal smeared genitals into it for durations of their slumber.

All sorts of things went through his head on the walk to the left of the dual carriage way. It was all usually about how much he was wasting his life in a house on his own doing a well paid but boring job as a computer analyst. He often wondered what would have happened in his life if he treated his girlfriends with more respect and dignity. Still, he hadn't and now he was lonely apart from his mates and the odd three minute wonders like he had tonight.

The next stretch of Boothferry Road led to a footbridge connecting two other roads without having to cross it, he could see a bright greenish light past the footbridge. It was moving slightly from side to side. He thought this unusual as almost every light down Boothferry Road was a mode of transport of some description, usually on its way to either the Humber Bridge or onto the M62 towards Leeds. He slowly walked closer, the light didn't grow or shrink in size which started to become disconcerting to Michael. It definitely wasn't a traffic light as it hadn't changed at all for the duration of him staring at it and it was swaying in the distance.

He crossed Anlaby Park Road South onto the next stage of Boothferry Road where the only path was a metre wide concrete path winding through the trees and bushes. He'd seen the light when the path swerved nearer the road so, as he was inquisitive he walked off the path and began to walk near the road off the concrete path and on the side of the road. His eyes were fixated on the light which still appeared not to change in size but continued to sway. The sensation of dizziness overpowered him and he slumped onto the grass at the side of the road.

Victoria had watched him as he had past her under the footbridge without knowing, where he thought the numbed pain he had felt on his arm was due to his drunken sway walking too near to the bridge's stanchions. It hadn't been that at all, it had been an injection but he as she watched him walk further across Anlaby Park Road South and down Boothferry Road, she thought that it had not worked until he began to sway. She raced as fast and as quietly as she could across the deserted road and onto the footpath that Michael has been using temporarily.

As the drug finally took hold of him Victoria walked over, grabbed his ankles and pulled him into the nearby bush which would hide them both. She sat next to Michael's limp body and looked down at him with disdain. People like him didn't even deserve to be born, never mind reaching the age that he has. This misogynistic loser represented most of the male population these days and the females just sat back and allowed this to happen, apart from her. She was strong enough to fight back against them, along with a few other thousand of them putting people straight about how women should be treated.

Victoria didn't just kill because men were misogynistic, she killed because she could and that she was far superior from anyone else on this small and lonely planet. No-one in particularly made her this way, she grew up and developed her own beliefs and feelings. This just happened to be the overwhelming belief that she had and she was determined to finish it before her time was up.

The idea of doing it on a larger scale did not appeal to her, she preferred to carry out her duties personally to make them feel special, at least once in their worthless lives. Children weren't part of her plan as they hadn't had the chance to prove themselves to her, only those that had made it to adulthood and not bothered to aspire to anything.

Laid in the leaves and evergreen of the bushes, Michael was in a pose that looked a lot like the swastika symbol. Victoria wanted to take her time but knew that she didn't have long. A noise in the nearby bushes halted her efforts momentarily but as soon as she knew she was safe she continued. However, someone was bound to pass or walk by walking their dog soon. The removal of his clothes was relatively easy as he wore things that wouldn't cling to his hefty figure. The weapon was relieved from her pocket and the hinge on it released. She teased it all over his body at first then sliced his wrists and femoral arteries with it. As his blood flowed into the foliage he did the only thing that would tell the Detectives that it was her kill. It wasn't the removal of his testicles as she had thought of originally, instead she looked as his thigh and carved Liam's name and a winking eye into it. They would know it was her now.

Chapter 19

Terry Hackett was sat with his laptop resting on his oak computer desk. Surrounded by acknowledgements of his achievements. He was the 'Killer Whisperer' and he was reading an email from another production company who wanted to follow him around on a case he was currently working on.

When he received the first request, his ego had gone into overdrive but soon realised that it would be strictly against his code. The code that was taught to him by a man he had visited whilst he was on the force in Liverpool. A man with such evil thoughts that he had turned himself in to the Police before his killing got 'out of hand'.

By out of hand he had meant more than two dozen University students who he had been teaching. He had watched them during the class, found out which dorm or flat they wee living in, stalked them, offered private tuition and then sliced off their limbs before eating their appendixes. No-one had suspected lovely Mr Taz, he was the nicest, most polite and helpful lecturer anyone student could have wished for. He decided to stop when his last kill was someone that he did not have any interest in killing but turned up at the wrong time at a friend's dorm room. The guilt he felt following the kill haunted him for two days before he casually walked into a local Police Station and confessed.

Terry had been in the building at the time and got the chance to have the initial interview. The man emptied his soul for seven hours and twenty three minutes. Providing Terry with information that no other killer had provided anyone with previously. It was true that killers had written books before or had a ghost writer do it for them, but none had truly spilled why they killed and what their processes really where.

Since that interview Terry has followed the code the killer had given him and he has had a 100% success rate as a Private Consultant to Police forces worldwide since.

He deleted the email from the production company and as he refreshed the inbox, another email appeared from a Police server address. He opened it and read what Wallis had to say. As Terry read on, he became more intrigued by every paragraph. By the end of the email, Terry had his mobile in his hand and was waiting to be put through to Wallis. He agreed that he would come and assist with their case but he needed certain assurances before he did.

1. He needed full control of the case, even over Wallis. Although he would let Wallis know what he was doing before he did it.

2. No back chat from any of the team when he orders or suggests something out of the box.

3. His own safe house within the City to live in for the duration of the investigation.

4. Copies of the entire case so he could read them extensively before he even arrived.

5. And finally, if Wallis took him off the case for any reason, he would still be paid in full.

Wallis agreed to all of his terms without hesitation and agreed for the files to be emailed over to him at the earliest opportunity. Terry told Wallis that as soon as his current case had concluded, he would make his way to Hull. He joked that he was currently in Budapest and that Hull would be a nice change, but Wallis who was a native Hullonian did not appreciate the tongue in cheek remark.

Meanwhile later that day Jan and Tim's bodies had been found by their daughter. She had received a phone call from both of her parent's managers asking if she knew where either of them were. She had let herself in and searched downstairs, it was only when she saw the bedroom door open and horrific sight inside of it that she knew what had happened.

Atkinson and Wallace knew that this would happen and as they pulled up outside of the house, they both looked at each other and knew that soon they would be subordinate to a man whose ego was so large it was pulling against the nearest black hole. Both mens body language told its own story, shoulders hunched over and slight leg dragging down the path of the victims. They looked like two school children who had been caught fighting and were on their way to the headmistresses office to have an hour long lecture about how much better it was to be friends than fight.

As Wallace opened the door to the house, they could hear Joyce's voice from upstairs and hoped that she didn't know of Terry's involvement in the case yet. Unfortunately for them, she did.

"Hello fellas, these two are a little bit different from the last ones." she informed them "These two have been de bowelled and pierced with what is believed to be the man's old butchers knives."

Both men looked at each other, bemused by the lack of quips and smart arse remarks but went along with it anyway. "But you still think this is our killer?" Atkinson asked her.

"Oh yes, most definitely. The same marks are here from the injections and the furniture is from the same warehouse too" both men nodding in agreement.

"The only thing is, the man has his genitalia but one of the woman's feet are missing." which caused Atkinson to sigh so loudly that his intake of breath almost caused him to be sick from the stench that the bodies were producing.

"I know, so expect it turning up soon wherever you may be. I will send a detailed report to Wallis as soon as I have finished." and got straight back to work, looking neither of them in the eye.

Wallace thought about it but regrettably asked the question.

"Are you okay Joyce?"

"No, I am not."

"What's up?"

"Before I came here I received a memo telling me that Terry Hackett was taking over the case soon and I am not a fan to say the least."

"Really?" Atkinson asked.

"NO! He is a pompous self absorbed sad state of a man who, in my opinion should be locked up himself for some of the techniques he uses to find the killers. And he takes credit for other people's work, acknowledging no-one but himself in catching them."

"But he has a 100% success rate" Atkinson replied.

"Oh so you carry a torch for him too do you? You two should be given more time on this in my opinion, but who am I to decide? I mean I'm only the sodding forensic expert."

"Woah there. What's all this?" Wallace asked and Joyce looked around at her team, the Officers and the two Detectives in the room.

"I'm saying nothing in here." she concluded and got back to looking at Tim's body.

"Can we talk lat..." Wallace requested but Joyce's right hand raised up towards him, halting him in mid sentence. "I'm busy."

"Joyce, downstairs NOW!" Atkinson ordered but she didn't move so he walked towards her. She stood back up and looked Atkinson straight into his eyes."

"In case you wasn't aware, you are no longer in charge of this case. Firstly I do not take orders from you and secondly, you need to get your arses into gear before Terry shows up and solves the case because of something you have overlooked. Am I clear enough for you?"

Atkinson's body slumped a little further over, walked out of the room, down the stairs and into the front garden. Wallace looked at Joyce, shook his head and followed his partner.

"She's right you know. That's the fucking worst thing about it."

"I know but it was out of order to say it in front of everybody."

"Lets just go back to the Office and speak to Wallis. I think I may ask for a transfer."

Chapter 20

Twenty days has passed since Atkinson told his partner that he was asking for a transfer. At after a heavy session in the local pub, talking with Wallace until the early hours, he had not only changed his mind but was more determined than ever to find the killer.

Unfortunately for both of them, still no clues had been found at the latest crime scene and as each day past so had their ability to see the case straight. Every angle they could think of was being followed. They had placed Officers watching the bedroom shop, the warehouse and any of the employees that could not provide sufficient alibis for any of the killings. Yet they still knew that time was drawing close to another bedroom murder being found.

As they sat waiting for the phone to ring, Joyce walked into their office without knocking first. Atkinson looked up at here.

"Haven't you heard of manners?"

"Why, were you sucking each other off instead of catching a killer again?" This made Wallace stand up and push Atkinson down into his seat before he even had the chance to stand himself.

"Calm down dough boys, I come in peace" and sat down next them. "Wallis just told me that Terry is on his way, arriving today or tomorrow. Now, I know that you two are the best Detectives that I have ever had the misfortune to work with and I know that you can crack this case. I know you both don't think that you can but believe me, everything you tell Terry will lead to him solving this case then he will receive all of the credit for it. Do you want that?" both men shook their heads and the three of them agreed to work together to make sure that everyone got what they deserved.

The entire team sat in the meeting room at 7.45am with Wallis sat at the front of the room.

"You all know why we are here so may I introduce you to Terry Hackett" his hand gesturing towards the door and as Terry walked through the door he actually began to clap. Some of the Officers and admin support followed along the clapping until he sat down next to Wallis.

"Please people calm down" Terry began. "I know I have made a name for myself but we are here to catch a killer. RIGHT!?" announcing at the top of his voice like he was addressing a self importance seminar. The room remained silent. All of the team had received a memo about how to deal with Hackett but Wallis had a one on one meeting with Joyce. Hence the reason why she had not stood up and asked whether this was the point we all orgasmed over him.

"I have read all of the case notes and I would firstly like to say that the leading two Detectives..." both Wallace and Atkinson held their breaths "...are the most professional duo I have ever read about in my entire career. I want to start by saying that neither of these two must have any blame for not being able to catch this vicious bastard. He is very good at what he does, but I am better." He stood in front of his peers, looking as if to receive another round of applause which was exactly what he was waiting for. When it never materialised, he invited the Detectives into 'his' Office which had formerly been theirs. Joyce could feel the trickle of imaginary blood leaving her lips as she bit them, stopping herself from comparing that ovation to one of Jimmy Saville turning up at an orphanage.

The three of them sat down and Terry pulled up a box onto the desk.

"This is the first case that..." looking at the notes for the names "...Marcus Grant and Thomas Willington investigated. We are going to go through each case with a fine tooth comb and see if anything pops up that didn't before."

"With respect Terry, we have been through these files hundreds of times but hit the brick wall each time." Wallace announced.

"But you haven't been through them with me have you?"

"No, but you say that you have read them. What else could we find if you haven't."

"Ah, I have made a list of questions to ask you in each case. This is going to take some time." Wallace and Atkinson glanced at each other and looked less than impressed. They remembered what Joyce had told them about them giving Terry the information, him taking the glory and the agreement that the three of them had made.

"May I suggest we ask Joyce Parker to join us, she is the lead forensic on all of these cases?"

"You may suggest that yes, and even better to have a woman's point of view around. Plus she can make us the drinks." which was met by a snort of laughter coming out of Terry's nose. The other two know however that she wouldn't take shit from anyone, especially him.

Terry called Wallis from the phone in his office and asked for Joyce to join them when she was free.

"So shall we start from when the bodies were found?" Terry asked "So we can put a picture together how this teenage couple were murdered."

Chapter 21

"Get your own fucking drink you sexist prick" Joyce blurted as she sat her buttocks down firmly to the hard plastic uncomfortable chair next to Wallace and Atkinson.

She had actually hurt her arse, she had sat down that hard but she was not going to reveal that to Terry. She continued, "If you have called me here to use my housework abilities whilst you all stroke cocks together, you have got the wrong woman. Barbara down there (she pointed to the office slapper) is the one you want. She will laugh at everything you say, make you whatever you wish and suck you off until you beg her to stop. Me, I am here because I am fucking good at what I do and my expertise is second to none. Kapeesh?"

"Fair enough Joyce" Terry answered looking at her in shock and taking a mental note of who Barbara was. "Let us know what you think, please."

"Well I think this sick individual has to know exactly what they are doing because of the lack of evidence. The time they must take to and not rush into just killing them must mean that they are so patient and are not just in it for the killing, they like to watch people too. Analyse why they deserve to die."

"Yes, I agree" Terry responded and Joyce looked at the other two with the look of 'see what I mean' on her face.

"They must also have been abused at some point n their life, you know with them removing the testicles on more than one occasion and leaving them for these two as a gift." Joyce stated, now lying to Terry so not to give him the satisfaction of catching the killer.

"Yes, he must have been but why take one of the last woman's feet?" Terry asked.

"They may have a fetish" Joyce answered.

"HE may have a fetish?" Terry corrected.

"Why HE?"

"Because it IS a he."

"How the hell do you know that this killer is a man?"

"Because it is"

"You are more sexist than I thought. This could equally be as much a woman than a man" trying to put that idea in Terry's head to take him, as Joyce thought, away from the killer. Little did she know that this sentence would take him closer to them instead.

As the uncomfortable silence hang in the air like a stale fart, a colleague burst into the room announcing that another body had been found.

"Where?" Atkinson asked.

"Down Boothferry Road" the colleague answered.

"What number?"

"No number, by the side of the road." Atkinson, Wallace and Joyce sat down. Terry and the colleague watched them quizzically.

"Why aren't you coming" Terry asked.

"Cos our killer only kills in people's bedrooms" Wallace replied.

The colleague coughed uneasily and spoke up "Liam Rowbotham's name and a winking eye is carved into the victim's leg just like his was."

All three of them jumped up and collided with each other as they did, trying to get out to the crime scene as quick as they could. Terry watched this farcical race and shook his head. What had he let himself in for?

....

At the crime scene now all suited up, Joyce was scanning the body and the immediate area around the body. She looked up at Terry as she was trying to work. "Is there a reason that you are just watching me?"

"No, just thinking"

"I told you, those thoughts are for people like Barbara" saying it in ear shot of Barbara who was taking the statement from the dog walker who had found Michael. Barbara turned her head towards Terry, which made him move away and pretend to look around the vicinity. 'Joyce wins again' she thought and smiled to herself.

Joyce called the three of them over just as the tent was being erected over the body. "He had sex not long before he died, I'll see if I can get some DNA off him just in case he was raped." Terry looked quizzical at Joyce, but before he could open his mouth Joyce opened hers.

"YES MR SEXIST, men can be raped too" she announced.

"I do know that you know. I was going to ask why rape someone at the side of the road when cars pass this area all of the time?"

"Well THEY killed him there, so why not rape him there too?"

Terry walked away from Joyce, towards Atkinson and Wallace.

"We need to get back and analyse this whole scene properly without any interference" pointing behind him to Joyce.

"Yes Sir, okay" Wallace answered and as they walked behind Terry Atkinson jabbed top in the ribs for his arse lickingly excruciating reply.

Chapter 22

Victoria watched with interest from one of the back bedrooms that looked onto the crime scene. She had come here yesterday hoping that someone would have found him but everyone just walked past, even the children going to the nearby school.

She recognised Atkinson and Wallace straight away from their encounters at the shop, but the woman prodding away Michael looked familiar too. The one person she knew immediately when she clapped eyes on him was Terry Hackett. His books on how he had caught previous serial killers were on her shelf at home, all bought at charity shops and car boot sales though, so not to have it on the system for someone to find. She was going to make sure that she was not one of those failed killers who appeared weak and predictable. She was cleverer than him and she was one thing a lot of killers aren't. Adaptable and that is why the person tied up behind her was going to die whilst the whole investigating team where a hundred yards away. Victoria had been in this house since disposing of Michael.

....

As soon as she finished carving his leg, a glance to her left revealed full view of a bedroom window from the houses that looked onto the wooded area at the side of Boothferry Road. The excitement began to build up as she thought of being able to see the chaos ensue from Michael being found until they took him away and forensic experts tried to look for clues. There was a fence separating the houses from the wooded area but thank fully for her, the council had yet to fit those metal spikey fences that they had promised four years ago, the fence were wire mesh with wooden panelling in some of the gardens that had bothered to create their own privacy.

It was still dark enough for her to move around without people being able to see her, and of course she would make as little noise as possible, like she always does. She clambered over the wire mesh, it actually making it easier for her to climb over with her small feet fitting into the holes. Her legs swung over the wooden panelling and she landed onto the grass on the other side of the fence.

The back of the house Victoria was met with consisted of an extension to the back of house, making the garden smaller but a good place for her to climb and gain entry to the back room upstairs. It not being upvc double glazed and a wooden frame would make it easier for her to gain entry. Her ear pushed up against the glass, listening for noises inside; snoring, talking, a television, anything. She heard nothing. This was the biggest risk she was about to take in all of her time doing her work.

As her head poked through the curtains of the room, she immediately saw that no-one slept in this room. It was a clutter room, a room where you store everything that really should be thrown away but you can't bring yourself to do it. Victoria knew that these houses were mostly three bedrooms so at most three people were potentially in this house. Two in the main bedroom and one in the other bedroom, all sleeping. She did not have time to check, she would just keep an ear out in case she was to hear any movements and a hiding place had already been spotted when she first looked around the room. Almost certainly no-one would even enter this room for quite long time unless they were placing something else in here that they could not throw away too.

A wooden ottoman was pulled up under the window and used as her seat whilst she sat there waiting for someone to find Michael's body. It wasn't the most comfortable of seats but the pay off of being able to see the furore of her work was worth every ache and pain sitting on it.

As the sun began to rise, dog walkers and runners sporadically past his partially covered body but none of them noticed him. As second hour past and quite a lot of people had past and still not noticed, Victoria was becoming more and more impatient with the next person who didn't see him.

After two hours and twenty four minutes of no-one noticing Michael, Victoria heard a noise from the room next to the clutter room. Her head turned away from Michael and towards the noise. Another noise made all of her senses switch to the other room and she totally focused as to what was happening. A few minutes of fumbling around and voices later, the person left the bedroom, walked past the room she was in and began to walk slowly down the stairs. Victoria silently walked towards to door and very carefully pulled it open. As she did she just saw the top of a head disappear out of sight. The hair was white and from the now clearer voice, she determined that it had been an elderly lady. The lady was talking to herself all the way down the stairs and Victoria could still hear mumbling once she was on the bottom floor of the house.

Sliding through a small gap in the door was a normal occurrence for Victoria, which she did with ease and silently walked into the room where the lady had come from. The door to the room was open and empty apart from furniture so she made her way to the only remaining bedroom of the house. That door was ajar and only a small amount of force was needed to open it. That room was empty but it did have a bed in, fully made up but looked like it had not been occupied for some time. Maybe this room was used when grandchildren came to visit or even a one of her children if they lived away.

Victoria returned to the clutter room, peeked out of the window for an update on 'Michael watch'; which was still fruitless and laid on the floor of the room trying to listen for noises below her. Victoria heard the noise of a television so she assumed that she still had quite a few hours before the lady would venture upstairs again, especially since her bed had been made.

Four more hours past of Victoria looking out of the window as person after person after person just walked past his body. She wished that she had not partially covered him now, but it seemed a good idea at the time. Not one dog had stopped to smell him or bark at his now decomposing body. She was used to everything going in her favour, so this setback was really testing her patience. She was going to sit here all day if she had to until someone found him, it was a good job she was not at work today, otherwise she would have had to find a telephone in the house and ring in sick from here.

Seven hours and nine minutes after she had climbed through this window, Victoria heard the lady unlock her front door and go out of it. She went to the front room window and saw the lady walking down the street. Whilst she could, Victoria raced downstairs and looked in the kitchen for something to eat but something that wouldn't make it obvious that someone had stolen it. She eventually found some crackers in the back of the cupboard along with a jar of jam. She scooped the jam onto the crackers one by one and ate enough for, what looked like a long stay in this house. Victoria also grabbed a glass from the drainer and drank five glasses of water. After the feast had finished, she checked that there was no evidence of her having been there and decided to return upstairs.

As her foot touched the first step, the telephone rang and actually made Victoria jump. It rang seven times and an automated answering machine message kicked in. After the beep came this message.

"Mum are you there? Mum? MUM! Pick up the phone, okay I am coming around in case you have wandered off again. Ring my mobile above this telephone if you hear this before I see you okay?" and a dial tone followed by "the other person has cleared" a few times before it cut off.

On hearing this Victoria ran up the stairs, quickly checked whether anyone had found Michael, which they hadn't and prepared a hiding place where this woman would not find her when she got here.

Within a few minutes the front door opened and closed quickly. "Mum, are you here?" she heard and then quick movements downstairs with the same call. When she had no luck downstairs, Victoria heard here rushing up the stairs. The person quickly checked over each room and found nobody. After she had poked her head in the clutter room

Victoria heard "Shit, why can't she just stay in the fucking house until I ring or get here?" come from the woman's mouth.

The front door opened again and slammed behind the woman as she left. She waited until she heard the car start and drive off before she came out from her hiding place. Victoria checked again on Michael to no avail which was beginning to really piss her off now.

Another three hours went by until the noise of shouting outside of the front door caught her attention again. Her gaze again moved from Michael and towards the noise. The front door opened and let in the noise with all of its glory.

"Now get inside and take your bloody coat off" was what Victoria heard, followed by "Okay, okay". As the argument progressed, it was obvious that the elderly lady was becoming forgetful, walking out of her house and getting lost. The daughter was obviously trying to control the situation, failing and finding it very stressful and a hard thing to cope with.

After the shouting had calmed down, Victoria could still hear them talking but even with her ear to the floor, she could only make out certain aspects of the conversation. Her gaze returned to outside of the window to the wooded area until she heard the daughter finally leaving the house. She left with the parting words. "So you understand why I am taking your house keys and locking you in then?", a pause followed by "You know that I am only doing this for your safety don't you?" The noise of the front door closing, locked and the sound of sobbing came from downstairs. The lady cried for a good few minutes and then began to walk up the stairs. Victoria moved to her hiding place as fast but as quietly as she could.

The lady walked into the clutter room talking to herself. "She has changed so much, I remember when she worshipped the ground that I walked on. Not any more." Victoria could she her looking through old photographs albums for a few minutes and all of a sudden looked up with a puzzled look on her face. "What was I upset about again? What was it? Was I upset? Maybe not, was I just remembering how life used to be? Yes, that's what it was."

Victoria watched as the lady took the photograph album she had in her hands and went downstairs with it. She took this time to look out of the window again and again feel disappointment at Michael not being found. She guessed that he had been as much of a failure in death as he was in life. As she turned her head, she saw a dog walk up to Michael's body and she looked intently for the next minute as the dog nudged, barked and even nibbled him a bit. Victoria looked up and down the area for an owner but there wasn't one to be seen. Was it her luck today that the only dog to find Michael was a stray? Her attention to the dog was soon interrupted by a cough from behind her.

Chapter 23

"Can I help you at all?" the lady asked and Victoria shook her head.

"What are you doing in my room?" she asked again, Victoria didn't say a word and a brief uncomfortable silence set in.

"Are you one of my imaginary people?" and without hesitation Victoria nodded.

"but you can't talk like the others?"

"Yes I can" Victoria whispered "but no louder than this."

"What are you doing here? Can I help you with anything?"

"Nothing thank you. I just want to look out of your window. Is that okay?"

"Of course, I'll go and make you a cuppa" and the lady turned around, walked out of the room and closed the door behind her. Victoria returned her attention to Michael for a good further twenty minutes before realising that the dark was going to come soon and she wouldn't be able to see anything from up here. A repositioning nearer him for a few hours at home for some sleep would be needed. The bedroom door opened and in walked the lady with a cup of tea.

"I am guessing that you are a two sugar person so I made the decision to put them in already. I hope you don't mind." Victoria shook her head, thanked her for the drink as she was so thirsty, even after drinking all of that water earlier and supped the drink down in one go.

"May I visit your lavatory please?" Victoria asked.

"Of course you may" the lady answered. How lucky was she that the only time she had let her guard down, she had been caught by someone who didn't know in the slightest if she was real of not.

The pain of taking off her kill suit just to visit the toilet was something she had thought hard about, hence why she hadn't been already. Putting the suit back on was equally as frustrating, she zipped up the front of the suit and the room became dizzy and her balance unmanageable. The door was forced open enough for her to crawl into the clutter room and see the lady in there, she was looking down at her smiling. All Victoria heard was "You didn't think I was that stup......" and all went black.

When Victoria roused and came to, she saw that she was alone in the room. A glance at the window showed that it was dark outside and there was no noise at all coming from the house. Victoria knew that the lady had no way of leaving the house; so either her daughter had collected her and left her be or the lady was hiding in the house somewhere.

Victoria stood up and, still feeling groggy, stood up with her hands using full cardboards boxes to steady herself. As the clutter room door opened, the noise from the television downstairs was of a familiar sound. It was the ten o'clock news theme and to confirm this, she heard the newscaster welcoming everyone to the programme followed by the half a dozen miserable headlines as usual. Her footsteps did not make a single sound in this house that was probably sixty plus years old, and peering around the corner of the door she could see the lady's head from the back watching the news. Victoria walked up behind her and before she choked the life out of her, the sound of snoring belted out of her mouth. Victoria smiled, walked back upstairs, rummaged through the plethora of boxes and grabbed items that she would need.

The return journey downstairs with the handful of items wasn't as quiet as the previous one but the slight noise still didn't disturb the still sleeping lady. As quick as a lightening strike the sellotape was wrapped around the lady's mouth until the breathing through her nose was loud enough to tell Victoria that she could both breathe and aware of what was happening. The extension lead that she had unravelled from it's holder was now being tied professionally around the lady's body, now laid on the floor in front of her chair and entangled in such a manner that the only limb she could move without pain was her head.

Victoria stood over the lady and whispered again "You have made the biggest mistake of your life not killing me when you had the chance." The lady's face looked puzzled as Victoria searched the room for identification of this lady. Eventually opened envelopes were found on the sideboard behind an ornament of a girl with two sheep. Her name was Beryl Watts and Victoria now had the information she needed to carry out her plan.

The dial tone from the telephone was audible from the distance she needed so no DNA could be found on it and she dialled the number above it on the white board. The number of Beryl's daughter. It rang until Victoria heard her pick the phone up and greet who she thought was her Mum ringing. When she didn't get an answer, she asked twice and shouted half a dozen times if her Mum was there. This was bound to work and Victoria knew that it would.

Kneeling in front of Beryl, Victoria told her that she was going to cut the sellotape away and if she shouting or made a loud noise, she would have to kill her. Beryl nodded her head, clarifying that she had heard the rules and felt the sellotape pulling out the small hairs from her top lip that she just couldn't get rid of.

"Your daughter is on her way and then I shall do my thing" Victoria told Beryl.

"Who are you?"

"I am not falling for that one again Beryl" she began but noticed the look in her eye after she had asked. Maybe she genuinely didn't know who she was, was that the only reason that she was still alive or not in Police custody. It was possible but it would mean that she would have to modify her plans. Surely the rest of her life with a deteriorating illness and no daughter to look after your well being was far worse than she could inflict on her.

The untying of the extension cable took little more than a few minutes and Victoria made a deal with Beryl. Her daughter for her freedom, which she kept telling her about until the lights from her daughter's car lit up the front room like a lighthouse.

The door opened in pitch blackness with the daughter shouting for her Mum. In the dark she could hear that the telephone was still in use with the same call that had made her come here. Not hearing or seeing any movement downstairs, she made her way upstairs to her Mother's bedroom. Just as instructed, as soon as Beryl heard her bedroom door open she walked out of the middle room, through the dining room and into the outside world. As she did this, her daughter about turned and walked towards the sound of the front door closing. Now in front of the clutter room, Victoria pounced on her from behind and choked her into unconsciousness.

Chapter 24

It was now 5.36am and the sun was just rising enough that the dog walkers and joggers would be out in force again soon. Her visit to Michael two hours ago ensured that someone would definitely find him and quick. As the first dog walked up to the body and began barking, Victoria knew that it wouldn't be long before she could look on at the people who were trying to catch her.

The reaction of the dog owner was not surprising but it was one she would never forget. She had not seen as much vomit leave an elderly man's mouth in her life. Firstly the Police officers arrived, followed by about ten plain clothed people. A lady crouched down at the body with her hood up, taking pictures and writing a lot of notes on pieces of paper in a folder. It wasn't until a good seven minutes had past until she saw the Terry Hackett and smiled to herself. She was going to look forward to getting one up on him.

Victoria waited until Hackett had left with Atkinson and Wallace then began to relax. If Hackett had been that good, she thought, he would have been looking for her watching the crime scene; and he hadn't.

The female who had been crouched over the body all the this time with her hood up, now stood up and turned around. Victoria couldn't believe her eyes that it was the same person whom she had been stood behind at the supermarket and who had made her cringe at her flirtatious advances to the shop owner. This time though, the woman's face was as serious at it could be. She was ordering other people about and eventually instructed the removal of Michael's body.

Once the tent had been taken down and the last of the forensic team had left, Victoria turned around and looked at Beryl's daughter (Rose was the name Beryl had told her).

"My time here has ended now and I need to get changed and off to work" Victoria informed her. A mumble came from behind the sellotape and her legs began to wriggle and writhe.

"Unfortunately that isn't a good thing for you is it?" and the woman shook her head and mumbled something else. All of the time Victoria had been watching them admire her work, she had been thinking of different ways of disposing of Rose. She still had her weapon so she could carve Liam's name and the eye on Rose somewhere, so they would know she had been watching. This excited her more than she had ever felt before but the risks she had taken had, in the end not been worth it and decided that she would not do it again in a hurry.

Rummaging around in the box only made the whole experience even worse for Rose but Victoria knew that she couldn't drag this kill out too far as she needed to be at work in just over ninety minutes.

Two heavy rock book ends came out of the box, clasped in Victoria's hands. Her smile towards Rose must have been maniacal as Rose's face drained of all blood as soon as she looked her in the eye. Like a sledge hammer the first book end hit Rose to the right side of her head, causing it to concave the skull in on itself. The second book end smashed down on Rose's face, hitting her nose to the bridge and connecting the upper lip and knocking teeth out of her now relaxed mouth.

A golden looking fluid exited from Rose's ears and nose and she laid motionless on the floor. Just to be sure, Victoria watched for any movement from the chest for a good two minutes before pulling out her weapon and carving Liam and the eye onto the body where only the forensic woman she'd seen at the shop could find it.

Victoria turned up for work on time having used some of Beryl's clothes, walking to a local shop, ordering a taxi to take her to the shops near her house, getting a quick shower and driving to work. She walked in to find Martin talking to a man in his twenties and a middle aged lady waiting to be seen. He gestured for Victoria to talk to the lady when she was ready.

After telling herself that she would protect her boss from becoming a suspect and carrying out her duties elsewhere, she changed her mind once she had finished speaking to the middle aged woman. Her name was Janice Wilton and her house was huge. She lived in a village on the outskirts of Hull called Swanland. She required her main bedroom completely renovating which was larger than the whole downstairs of Victoria's house and then some. The layout of the room was just too tempting to turn it down in her head.

It wouldn't be ready for a good few weeks yet, even though she was prepared to pay over the odds for her room to overtake others in the queue. There was a lot she could do in that time to drag the incompetent Detectives thoughts from even thinking about Martin being a suspect until she began watching Judith.

Even so, the thought of being free to roam in that room, watching her routines and then disposing of her, made a tingle shiver down Victoria's body from the base of her skull to the end of her toes.

First though, would be a visit to the Humber Bridge.

Chapter 25

Damien was a keen running enthusiast. He had taken up the sport as a hobby, continuing his success as a long distance runner at school. He was a very awkward person who wasn't the most competent or intelligent of people, so when he found something that he was good at, he ran with it.

Even though he was successful with his running at school, he was not revered as other pupils were. Instead the other pupils laughed at the way he ran. Everyone has their own unique style of running but Damien looked like he was about to both follow through after an enormous flatulence problem and that he was trying to scrape something off the bottom of his trainers. The children couldn't wait for P.E (Physical Education) in order to see him run. That is all Damien was allowed to do and the letters to his teachers from his parents told them exactly that. They didn't want him swimming due to his short stature in all departments and he had a fear of being submerged. He was not allowed to partake in group sports as he was always the only to be chosen last and the person everyone blamed for their team losing. His parents had always shielded him from others when they first found out that he was different to other children. He was always more socially unskilled and not able to grasp higher than basic comprehension of tasks.

Of course, the better thing for them to do would have been to allow him to behave and act like a normal child instead of wrapping him up in cotton wool. After school life Damien tried to go to college but his academic inadequacies would get in the way yet again. He spent a total of four weeks there before his parents received a call from the course tutor already, knowing that Damien didn't have what it took to pass the level one course in Sports Science.

Instead he became a member of a local running club who only looked upon him for his running prowess and nothing else, and he got himself a full time job stacking shelves in a locally owned supermarket. The same one where Victoria and Joyce had met for the first and penultimate time.

As Damien's running improved he would enter himself into races locally and would do very well in them. However like everything he did, his parents weren't too far behind him, wanting him to push himself further and hounded him to become in charge of the running club. This was not an easy task for him to achieve as at just over five foot, his presence with other runners was like a gecko looking up at an elephant's foot about to squash him.

The only other way he could think of becoming dominant and to please his parents was to spread rumours about the person in charge of the club sneakily. Eventually and after a year of persisting emails from an 'anonymous' source, the person stood down from the club. Other people in the club just simply did not have the time to take the responsibility of running a club on, so at a meeting Damien was voted in as the only standing candidate.

Now as previously mentioned Damien is inept and incompetent, however his parents weren't. They advised Damien to delegate almost all of the tasks out to other members of the club and just sit back and relax, allowing everyone else to do his work. His attitude to new members who saw what was going on was appalling, he would basically make them feel so unhappy, they would eventually leave. His 'Napoleon Complex' found in most small men was hidden well from people who knew him well and who he had a hold onto, but obvious to those who attempted to take away anything away from him.

Every Wednesday night after his shift at the supermarket he would run from work to the Humber Bridge Country Park, run around it and then run home. This run was easy for him as he was used to running many Marathons and even run to his hotel after it. This particular night it was darker than usual due to the very cloudy night and the almost disappearing crescent of the moon. The Country Park has four trail paths, some including stairs and other routes did not. It had been a quarry in the past but the local council had seen its potential and turned it into a park.

Victoria had been here lots of times before to collect her thoughts, with dates and taking on a good run herself. She knew exactly where to position herself in order to make the most impact and the best way to accomplish her objective. At 7.53pm she spotted a fluorescent jacket bobbing towards her.

On a part of the course where the gradient was 1:3, Victoria placed herself at the bottom of the slope on the floor holding her ankle and as Damien approached the top of the slope he saw her. He shuffled slowly down asking her if she was okay.

"I think that I have twisted my ankle"

"Okay, let me get down there and take a look" and he crouched down to look at her leg. As he got closer he recognised her.

"I kn.kn.know you don't I? You work at the bed shop near where I work"

Truth be told, he had quite an obsession with Victoria. He would look for her inside of the shop every time he passed it but never dared go inside to talk to her. He knew that she was totally out of his league and the fact that he still lived with his parents, so he had no say whether he needed a new bedroom or not didn't give him a reason to go inside.

Now having her exactly where he was running and not being able to run due to hurting her ankle, was precisely the situation he needed to take advantage of her predicament.

"Do you want me to help you up" Damien asked.

"Sure but be careful, it really hurts." Damien put his arm around Victoria's waste and her arm around his shoulder. "After three I am going to lift you up and then you stand and rest on me, okay?" Victoria nodded and hummed in agreement. He stood her up and she leaned against him, causing him to really put a lot of effort into helping her. Fifty yards down the path she stopped, turned to him and whispered in his ear "How can I ever repay you for helping me?" Damien sniggered like a teenage boy and replied "I am sure I can think of something."

"So can I" and she plunged her weapon into the side of his neck. Damien let out a loud scream holding his hands against the wound, blood spurting and seeping through his fingers. He looked at her and tried to ask why she had done this, him now weakened onto his knees. Victoria crouched down, looked him deep into his eyes "Aw don't feel special because you aren't. You were just the first person to come along and try to take advantage of me, you sad little shit." On hearing the word 'little' Damien found some more energy from somewhere and lunged at Victoria, sadly for him his incompetence struck again as he slipped and landed face first onto the weapon still being held in her hand. The blade entered through the bridge of the nose and as Victoria looked down and him, she could just see the tip poking out of the back of his head.

She let go of the weapon, kicked his now limp body over onto his back, placed her foot on his neck and pulled her weapon back out. The squelch made a satisfying sound that at first she wanted to make again but she knew that time was against her in a public place. She wanted him to be found a lot quicker than Michael was so she carried out her pre thought plan, although she wouldn't be sticking around to see the aftermath of this one.

Victoria finished and glanced up at her handy work. Not bad for a skinny, petite woman but he wasn't much of a man was he? She walked out of the Country Park, got into her car and drove home.

He stepped out of one of the surrounding bushes when he heard her car pull away. He looked up at her work, smiled and left.

Chapter 26

Joyce arrived at the crime scene and looked up "Looks like he ran into some difficulties" she said to the Officer next to her followed by a nudge into his side. The Officer showed no reaction and neither did any of the rest of the team around her. "Jesus, what's up with you lot? 6.27 Monday morning blues or something?". "No" replied the Officer "It's because there is a mutilated dead body hanging from a tree in this park and we are sick of this shit happening here, yet you seem to want to make a joke all of the time."

Joyce stood right next to the Officer and leaned in against him. "Listen to me, if I didn't make jokes and poke fun, I would be a hell of a lot crankier than I am about to be after this sentence. In my job I see dead bodies every day, some of them I can't even help post mortem because of some sick fuck using this area as a twisted garden of death. You understand?" she pulled away from the Officer and said louder "Now get your dick out if we all really want to laugh" and winked at him.

The Officer just stood, took it like a man and continued to monitor the area. Two other Officers were carefully cutting Damien down and as soon as his body touched the ground, Joyce raced over to see what she could. The puncture wound to the head and neck were obvious but she was looking for anything more obscure. "You two stay here" she told the Officers "I am about to take off his trousers, the Officers looked at each other. "It's okay I'm not a perv, well I am but not in this situation." Down came the compression trousers and Joyce checked both legs, no markings were there. She checked the genitalia area and although it looked like it at first, the testicles had in fact not been removed they were just tiny, like small milky marbles. Checking around the groin area for the killer's marking or anything else but she found nothing.

Joyce sighed and asked for her colleagues to place him in the bag for transportation, and as they turned him over she spotted it.

Liam's name and two kisses had been carved into his right buttock.

Between her phone call and the arrival of Hackett, Atkins and Wallace; it had been fifteen minutes, in which time Joyce had already secured the area and took samples of some material she had found around the area. After she had explained what she had found, Atkinson and Wallace sighed so loudly it moved Hackett's side parting. Hackett turned around and looked at them both. "Giving up so early I see."

"No" Atkinson answered back with a snap in his voice "It's just that these last two have been completely away from the norm. Every other murder that we have found has been performed in a bedroom bought from the same shop and made at the same place."

"So?" Hackett replied and Atkinson shrugged his shoulders. "So, it probably means that you got close when you investigated last time and now he is trying to throw you off by killing elsewhere." Atkinson walked away and mumbled something about losing his touch and should have seen that himself. Wallace followed him as Joyce approached Hackett.

"They have been on this case so long that I think it is frazzling their minds" she stated.

"It just needs a fresh pair of eyes. I have been in plenty of cases where I didn't have the foggiest idea what was going on, asked for help and they saw something I didn't." Joyce looked up at him, surprised that he had admitted that he too had foibles, "Who the fuck do you ring when YOU don't know what the hell is going on?"

"I only trust a handful of others and none of them are from this country. We aren't at that stage now, I am going to visit the warehouse and the bedroom shop myself and let them two get their head straight. Let them know for me please" and Joyce nodded. Hackett walked over to his hire car BMW and set off. Atkinson and Wallace watched as he drove off and Joyce told them what he had said.

Looking through the old files in his car, Hackett wanted to be sure that his gut instinct was correct before he went inside. He had already spent over two hours at the warehouse and not had a feeling on anyone. That only left one more place to visit. He looked into the shop and saw them both talking to customers. Neither of them knew him so he would pretend to be a customer.

He walked through the door and neither of them looked up at him. Too fixed on the computer screens with their respective customers going through different designs. Hackett could hear the normal sales patter to try and get them to spend a little more and then a little more; making it sound like the deal is too good to be true. He waited until he could hear the end of one of the deals and turned to look at who he thought was the manager. "I will be with you in one minute Sir, thank you for waiting" Martin told him. Hackett had looked deep into his eyes when he had been acknowledged but didn't see any recognition at all.

After a few minutes Martin gestured for him to sit down and Hackett and for the next twenty five minutes he made up a room that he wanted refurbishing, constantly watching for signs of acknowledgement in his body language. Hackett was watching so closely that he only just noticed Victoria's hand being placed on Martin's shoulder as she said goodbye at the end of her working day. Hackett looked her up and down, admiring her and wondering what he could do in just a short time alone with her.

His eyes followed her out of the door, again admiring her from behind. As the door closed, she turned around and looked him straight in the eye. Hackett snapped out of the stare embarrassed at being caught and returned his gaze back to Martin.

At the end of the conversation & not taking the deal that Martin had offered, even almost gone down to base price to try and change his mind, Hackett stood up, shook Martin's hand and left the shop, taking one last look at him as he left.

Hackett drove to his hotel car park and began to take notes on his visit, writing every single detail down before he forgot some of it. When he finished, he concluded that in his opinion, Martin was not who they where looking for either. He wrote 'Back to the drawi' when he received a text. One look at the phone told him that it was Joyce. The text read 'We want to talk to you about the case. We need to stick together, you know I am right.' He replied 'Ok I am on my way. Yes you are usually right aren't you?' and hit send.

All of a sudden, an electrical spark went off in his mind. It all fell into place, every single of piece of it. How could he have been so idiotic and blind? He picked up his phone and typed *'Joyce was right, it is a woman. It's'* was all he could tap out until he felt something on his neck and Victoria whispering into his ear "Shhhhhhhhh, just drive. I already have your weapon and now I have your phone."

Chapter 27

Hackett could feel the acid in his stomach bubbling and working its way to his sphinctoral muscles in his anus as the blade, which must be have been sharp due to him feeling a trickle of blood slide down his neck onto his chest, was pressed against his femoral artery.

"You are too late" he whispered "That text has already been sent."

"No, it hasn't. I grabbed it from you before it could send."

"Do you really think that I didn't know you were there? I am a famous Detective who catches people like you every day of the year. Of course I sent it." Victoria reaches behind her were she threw the phone down and grabbed it, slightly knicking Hackett's neck as she stretched. She looked at the still pre sent text not yet sent.

"No it hasn't, it is still on the screen."

"GOOGLE, SEND TEXT!" Hackett shouted and off it went into the cyber ether. 'Sent' it read, underneath the message. She dropped the phone, grabbed Hackett by the neck and made in incision underneath his jaw. "That was a fucking stupid thing to do, don't you think?"

"Not really no. She will get what I mean eventually and they will be coming for you Victoria."

"Who is she?"

"A woman more than capable of putting that half text together and sending the whole force after you."

"But you will be dead."

"I have had too many close shaves to give in to that thinking now. Besides, if it means that they get you and it stops you, that's all that matters."

"You would give your life just so I could be caught?"

"I already have, for you and those just like you."

"Very well, you are going to take me up to your hotel room and that is were you shall die, in the bedroom."

"How fitting." Hackett replied and the force on her sticking his neck with the blade made him open his door and exit the car.

"Obviously I can't hold this against your neck as we walk in but put your arm around me like we are drunk and walk me to the lift. I will have the blade on your spine the whole time. Understand?"

"Of course."

Hackett did as she asked even though when they walked through the reception, there was no staff member at the desk. The act continued in the lift and then out of the lift and into his hotel room.

"Sit on the bed" Victoria ordered and he did. "Can I just ask you one question before you kill me, seeing as though I am going to take the answer to the grave with me?"

"What?" she answered with a sigh of tiresome after it.

"Why?"

"Why not."

"That is the lamest answer I have ever heard from anyone I have caught."

"But you didn't catch me, I caught you."

"Touche Victoria, touche."

"Surely you want to tell somebody why you killed all of those people."

"Not really, why should I? It is no-one else's business but mine, so why should I want to tell anybody, especially you?"

"You see the thing is, I know you do want to tell me. And no-one else will ask you until you are being interrogated. So why not just tell me now and then it will be out of your system."

"You are so sure that they will catch me aren't you?"

"I am now yes."

"How come?"

"Well, that text was sent about fifteen minutes ago and it won't take her long to realise what I meant by it. Where is one of the first places they are going to send Officers to search?"

"Here."

"Yes. Wait, you want them to come don't you?"

"Yes." she answered with a wry grin on her face. "And you are right, I do want to tell someone why I do it."

"Go ahead, I won't judge. I have heard all sorts of reasons, I am sure yours will be no different." Victoria moved a chair opposite Hackett as he sat on the edge of the bed, she sat on it and leaned back.

"I do this" she whispered, making Hackett move forward to listen "because I like it" and within a millisecond her right leg swung up and kicked Hackett right under his nose, making him fall the her right and onto the floor. While he was down there her right foot connected with his genitals twice before he curled up into a ball to protect them.

Victoria walked back to the chair laughing. "Gullible arsehole."

Like a switch, rage filled Victoria's body like it was being pumped intravenously into every possible injection point in her body. She rushed over to Hackett, laid on top of him, grabbed his jaw between her left hand pincering his cheeks together and the blade in her right hand right above his heart.

"Someone made me like this. Just the once was all it took, just the feeling of ending one person's life as a favour gave me the lust for it. Why shouldn't I fucking do it? The World is full of ignorami and people who piss away their lives without a thought to those who can't provide life or feel pleasures like others feel. Why should they be allowed to live when people who have life threatening illnesses beg each night to be given a second chance or people kneel before a statue of a crucified symbol in the vain hope that the network of people involved in that community can make them a better person? Why should people who take everything for granted or are given everything from birth have a better chance or surviving than someone who has been brought up in squaller and had to kick and fight for everything they have? EH!? WELL FUCK YOU MR 'I WANT TO KNOW WHY YOU DO IT' FUCK. YOU."

The blade slid into Hackett's chest wall like it was made of blancmange. The sound of the blade puncturing his heart made Victoria go all tingly and she felt a shudder of nerves prickle all the way down her back. The blade lifted out of his body and a jet of blood sprayed out of the wound and up against the ceiling of the hotel room, missing Victoria totally. When the sprays subsided she leaned forward and put her mouth against his left ear. "So now you know eh? Just one thing, you will have to ponder in your dying moments whether what I told you was real or bullshit. You will never know, and that is why I win again."

Victoria stood up, looked down on the poor excuse of a man and spat on him. What did she have to lose? She knew that they knew now, this was her confirmation to them. She would have like to scrawl Liam's name on his leg but she knew that time was short. Her D.N.A would be enough.

From the purposely made woodland area in front of the hotel car park; she watched as one patrol car pulled up outside of the hotel, the Officers got out and then five minutes later, another half a dozen cars and vans turning up with loud sirens. Joyce, Atkinson and Wallace got out of the car at the front and walked into the hotel. Now Victoria knew who SHE was, she was the same person who was looking at Michael on Boothferry Road and the same person who was flirting with the supermarket owner. She would be the last as Victoria now understood how important she was.

Chapter 28

"Holy fucking shit" left Joyce's mouth. "I can't believe that she actually killed him". She paused for a few seconds, taking in the crime scene. "Fucking bitch".

Atkinson and Wallace just stood, hands in their pockets, staring at Hackett's dead body with Joyce prodding, poking and removing his clothes.

"Funny that he wanted me to do this when he was alive, but now here I am doing it post mortem".

"Yeah, fucking hilarious Joyce" Wallace replied.

She examined his entire body but Liam's name or any other marks were not visible. Joyce stroked her chin, wandering why she hadn't left her 'calling card' for them.

"You feeling your beard?" Atkinson quipped to Joyce.

"No, I am checking if any of your wife's pubes are still stuck to my face". Wallace bent over holding his stomach, laughing uncontrollably.

"Funny bastard" Atkinson replied and Joyce bowed theatrically.

"So why didn't she leave her squiggle guys?"

"Maybe she didn't have time" Wallace answered.

"Maybe it wasn't her" Atkinson stated.

"Who else would it be numb nuts? Christ, no wonder you couldn't see her in plain sight every time you visited that shop".

"Fuck you clever cunt, FUCK YOU! Don't you think that we feel guilty enough not picking up that she was the killer without you mentioning it?"

"Oh I don't doubt that you feel guilty, however guilt isn't going to save anyone else, especially now that it seems that she knows that we know. She may even go into hiding, never kill again or move elsewhere and start afresh".

"Oh she'll kill again Joyce, I know she will" Wallace announced. "How can you not when you have killed the famous Hackett and got away? When she does she will slip up somehow. Plus, now we know who she is, she can't get far without someone seeing her".

Atkinson stared out of the hotel room and looked into the distance, thinking about all of the families of those people Victoria had killed. All mourning the deaths of their loved ones who had only wanted new bedroom furniture. He remembered each and every family member he had met, including the mother who was attached to an oxygen tank and had to be hospitalised due to the news. He remembered going to see her when she was recovering, he remembered...... did he just see her in the bushes?

He looked closer, examining each clump of shrubbery surrounding the area. He was sure someone was lurking behind them. Atkinson reached down for his radio and called down to an Officer who was stood outside of the hotel. Upon speaking into his radio, he saw the black blur race out from behind the bushes and away from the hotel.

"Fuck me, she's outside!" he shouted. Wallace, who was sat on one the chairs in the room jumped up like he had been electrocuted and raced out the door, crashing into Atkinson as they both tried to leave through the doorway at the same time.

Atkinson was bellowing into his radio about where he had seen Victoria without trying to shout too loud so he would be inaudible but enough so the Officers could hear him.

Both Detectives left the building and Atkinson pointed into direction in which he saw her flee. Wallace ran to the car and caught up with Atkinson, stopping so he could get in the passenger side. They really had no idea which way she had gone but they weren't going to give up now.

The helicopter had been called and was on its way to the area but really, there were lots of people about, she could have got along way by now. She could have even got into a car and sped far away. This wasn't going to stop either of them though. Such trivial things would not stop them until all hope was lost.

The helicopter had noticed a figure laid on a road close by and Officers were on their way towards them. Maybe she could have been ran over whilst getting away, or maybe....

"It's a dead male" the radio announced. "Neck slit from side to side Sir".

Wallace banged his hands on the steering wheel "Fucking hell, FUCK.ING.HELL". Everyone began to converge on that area now; especially the helicopter who was now looking for anybody hiding, crouching behind bins, fences, back gardens and under cars.

The Officer in the helicopter radioed down, saying that a person appeared to be hiding behind some industrial bins. The whole team bar two cars converged on the area, but not too close.

Wallace and Atkinson got out of their car around the corner from the bins and walked slowly with their weapons at the ready. Each detective approached the bin from either side, Wallace took the lead and when the signal came they flung the bin away from the wall and shouted at the person crouched down.

"Stand up slowly with your arms above you head" Atkinson ordered.

"I'm sorry, I'm so sorry" the female replied, not Victoria but they didn't know that yet.

"Just do what he says. NOW!" Wallace barked at her.

"I can't" was the reply. "She tied my arms down the side of my body". Not knowing whether this was a trick or not, Atkinson shone a torch into the woman's face, only to find out that it was indeed not Victoria. He lowered his weapon and shook his head at Wallace, indicating that it was not her.

"Bollocks!" Wallace announced in front of everyone. "Where did she go then?"

"She told me to close my eyes" the woman began "She said that she was going to stay right next to me and if I opened them, she would cut them out. I thought you were her at first putting on a voice until I heard more than one of you".

"That's just great" Atkinson shouted and pushed the woman towards a female Officer.

They searched the area for another two hours or so until the both of them finally gave up and returned to Joyce with the bad news.

....

The satisfaction of watching the proceedings of her work, especially to someone as well renowned as him filled Victoria full of adrenaline again. If she wanted to, she could massacre them all right now but they would be too easy and when has she ever chosen that path?

Watching all three of them stood in the hotel room mouths aghast; not truly believing what they were seeing was heightening her satisfaction levels through the roof. Killing those three would be even more pleasurable and she knew who she would leave until last.

Her.

She needed to get closer to the patrol car to see if she could swipe something that would aid her in her pursuit of them. She had watched loads of TV shows were the Police car doors were always open and there was always something handy inside to use. Sadly as soon as she moved, she saw that she had been noticed. A different type of adrenaline now kicked in, she needed to get away as fast as she could and in a direction that wouldn't be too obvious.

Regrettably with her being on a hotel complex, there wasn't much room for movement in which exit she could choose. She clearly hadn't thought this bit through had she?

Her legs were moving exactly where her eyes were pointing. Everywhere where she shouldn't be going, she was. She had to think where they would think she was going and go where they wouldn't. All of this and being sure that no-one saw her either was really testing her senses.

As she flew around a corner, she noticed a man walking slowly towards her about ten yards away. In the time it took her to reach him, her weapon was out of its holster, slicing his throat and her legs had already passed him before he contemplated what was happening to him.

Now she would have to deviate from her current path even more because he would be found sooner rather than later.

Approaching the shops, she slowed down and as she did noticed a woman leaving the convenience store ahead. If she sped up a little bit, but not too much, she would reach her right next to those bins. Which she did.

With her hand over the woman's mouth, she gave her specific orders what she could and couldn't do. Stealing her coat was one of those things, and it was even better that she was wearing everything black underneath her coat. Victoria put her coat on the woman, it didn't meet in the middle but that didn't matter and gave her further instructions.

She watched from the house down the road as Wallace and Atkinson approached the bins. Choosing this house was easy. There was a front garden big enough for three cars but no cars on the drive, the front room curtains were open and no lights were on inside. Now either someone too young to drive was asleep on their own or the house was empty. Tonight she had to take that gamble as she couldn't go home again. Tonight she was lucky.

After fifteen minutes, Victoria watched as the Detectives drove past the house and Officers followed on foot looking in the gardens. None of them saw her watching them.

Chapter 29

Once Victoria knew that she was safe from the Police, she tried to figure out how long she could stay in this house for.

Turning the computer and scouring it for any evidence was relatively easy. An encrypted email address with emails still in it, once she has spotted them among the spam, where from a company who rented out Cottages in Cornwall. From the dates on the emails it appeared that Victoria had six days in the house interrupted, that was unless someone was checking the house for them whilst they were away. Victoria suspected that her neighbours were just going to keep an ear and eye out for them. There had been no stupidly secreted key under a stone or in a nearby bus that she had found, so her suspicions were correct as far as she was concerned.

While she was on their computer, she remotely logged on to her works email. She knew that they would be checking if she did, so she downloaded a piece of software to show that she had actually accessed it from home. That would confuse the hell out of them. Good job that she knew her own I.P address. Using her emails, she printed out every single address of all of the people who she had done business with but not 'met' yet, together with the plans of the bedrooms they had ordered. After she had them all, she deleted her entire email history.

Knowing full well that they would access her work computer, which they could be already, she logged into that too and deactivated all of her jobs and past messages regarding the bedrooms ordered.

She wasn't stupid, she knew that the Detectives would be able to find out which jobs she had taken by visiting the factory again. However since their last visit didn't end very well with one of their employees, Victoria couldn't see them giving up the information quickly; especially since she was loved, lusted after and respected by all of the workers there.

Once she had completed everything she needed to do, the bathtub with a spare pillow was to be her bed. It would be easy to get rid of her DNA and the bathroom was at the top of the stairs from the front door so she could hear if anybody was coming in. The bathroom was also good because if you are checking someone's house for them, who realistically checks the bathroom or uses it?

Once she had awoken, Victoria figured out that she more than likely had five days to complete another kill before having to start again somewhere else. She had been sloppy with Hackett and she knew that she was going to have to pay for it now. The name Kirsty had always been popular with her, that is what her new name would be. Kirsty Mullgallon.

Firstly she needed to choose which person she was going to rid the world of followed by the Detectives when they came for her and finally, HER.

Sifting through the lists of bedrooms, whittling it down from over a dozen to three. The three she had kept were the only ones that she could possibly do within the time period she was bound to. That in itself was going to be restricted once the Detectives got hold of the list too, but she did have her hiding places that substituted for air pockets and other various guises inside of the furniture if any Police Officers or the Detectives came looking.

The list finally came down to one person, one bedroom. A bedroom so large she could probably fit most of her house inside of it. The bedroom of Janice Wilton, a well to do lady who wanted her bedroom to look like it was expensive but done as cheaply as possible. Victoria had admired her honesty by telling her straight what she wanted without making some lame excuse to go around the houses to make the same point. Now the only thing Victoria was going to admire was the way that she was going to die.

....

Atkinson, Wallace and Joyce sat in Wallis' office.

Wallis had his right hand caressing his brow, moving his fingers together and stretching them out, attempting to ease the current headache that he had.

"Right, were are we?" Wallis looked up to see Joyce open her mouth "Cram it Joyce". Her mouth closed looking disappointed but realised that now was probably not the time.

Atkinson piped up, shaking his head at Joyce "Well we have got hold of her boss and Wallace is meeting with him first thing in the morning..."

"Why are you not there now?" Wallis asked and stared at him. "Because Sir, he is not available until then".

"Not fucking available" Wallis' head now bubbling inside "Get out of here, ring him and tell him to get his arse down to the shop and give you everything that you need. Understand?" Wallace nodded embarrassingly and walked towards the Office door.

"What's wrong with you three, has this case mushed your fucking heads? For fucks sake" and his office door slammed as Wallace left the room.

"Now you" pointing at Atkinson "I want you to go to the warehouse and go through every bedroom she has commissioned and tear those plans apart and follow up every single one of them that has been completed." Atkinson nodded too.

"As for you Joyce, you have been the only solid one in this department. Take a team, a big team to her house, scour that place and find me everything that I need to convict her. I will head a team to look for her, I am now in charge of this case."

....

Victoria watched as her hair changed colour from the bleach and after she had cut it short. She removed every piece of make up from her face and put on some clothes that she found in one of the bedrooms. They wouldn't keep her away from public eyes but it was something completely different from what she wore normally. She would be hiding in plain sight but it would also help her getting to where she needed to be.

Chapter 30

Victoria left the house by the back door, scaled the fence once she had checked that no-one was looking, walked down the ten foot and onto the street.

There she was, bleached blonde hair, glasses that she had found in a cupboard and didn't hurt her eyes. She was hoping it would have the Clark Kent affect, a short pink and yellow skirt which would probably show the tips of her buttocks if she bent down, a white boob tube with her black bra underneath showing through the top, a red sleeveless denim jacket that she had left unbuttoned and these god awful animal pattern high heeled shoes making a racket every time her foot touched the ground.

It was totally not what she would usually wear and would attract the attention of as many people as possible, but she needed to do for more than one reason.

The Police and the Detectives would be looking for someone who was trying to evade them and not draw unequivocal attention to herself, which she more than was doing. Plus, if she was dressed like this, she knew that she would be able to access the house that she so desperately needed to be in.

Victoria knew, from researching her, that Janice Wilton liked young women. She would scour the night clubs for young women, have her way with them and pay them to fuck off and never return. She was a loner who just required her sexual needs fulfilling and nothing else. She hadn't built her empire from having to worry about a partner that would only add undue stress to her life. Unattached sex with young women was good enough for her and if she failed at those attempts, she would consider taking a man home. Failing that, she had plenty of other things that would satisfy her but they were only as a last option.

Janice wasn't an unattractive woman, she knew how to dress to attract people's attention. In her mid forties, she tried hard to make herself look at least ten years younger and a lot of people had commented to her that she did indeed look in her thirties. Those however were the people she was about to have sex with, so not exactly an unbiased opinion, she always thought but didn't really care as a compliment is a compliment no matter in what form.

Roaming the streets for a few hours, getting on buses and even walking within a hundred yards of her house with the Police surrounding the area, even though they thought that they were well hidden, was satisfying to her that nobody had recognised her but a lot of people had looked at her. She had felt all of those eyes looking at her slender figure but showing the right bits of it off. She had stopped off near Janice's house and walked all around the perimeter of it. Tempted though as she was, she would wait and she whether tonight was one of those nights Janice needed satisfying. If it wasn't, Victoria only had four more nights left to do what she needed to. It wasn't her normal way of ridding the world of someone, she would of course loved to have lay in the pockets of open space for a few weeks, watching Janice's life roll by before the right time came to finish her off.

At nine o'clock that even Victoria positioned herself more or less outside of Janice's house but not too close so it wouldn't look obvious that she was waiting for her.

The gates began to move and she knew that Janice would be coming past in a few seconds in her chauffeur driven car. Victoria stood almost but not exactly opposite Janice's field of vision pretending to be on her mobile phone in the middle of an argument. As the car past Victoria she looked up, staring right at Janice making sure that she could see everything she had to offer and smiled directly at her whilst still in the middle of this made up conversation. The car drove past her and disappeared into the distance. She had failed but she still had four more nights to try and if that didn't work she would just have to dress in her kill outfit and do it old style but crammed into one night, which she didn't really want to do.

Victoria walked back to the bus stop and looked at the timetable, there wasn't another bus for about forty five minutes so she got on her phone to ring a taxi. As the operator answered Janice's car pulled up beside her, Victoria immediately swore into the phone.

"You'll have to fucking wait now cos some gorgeous woman has pulled up beside me and wants me. At least someone does." Victoria pretended to hang up the phone. "Yes love can I help you?"

"Why don't you forget about that waste of space on the phone and come with me for the best night out you will ever have."

"Wow, you're a bit forward aren't you?"

"Yes I am but you never get anything as delicious as you if you don't ask do you?"

"Suppose not. Where are you off?"

"We will be going to the Fireworks club on Wright Street then back to mine, does that sound okay?"

"How do I know that you aren't some sort of freak or if he (pointing to her chauffeur) is your husband and he loves to watch us or something?"

"You see that house?" as Janice pointed down the street "That is where I live, I was going to offer you to come straight into my home but thought that you would like a good time first. This man is my chauffeur and I am not married (she showed Victoria her hand), look no ring and no white mark either."

"Sure, why not." the door opened and Victoria climbed inside "We don't need to go to Firework first you know" and she grabbed hold of Janice's inside thigh. Janice smiled, looked into Victoria's eyes and told her driver to drive home. Victoria saw his eyes roll into the back of his head and heard a slight sigh come from his mouth.

The car drove through the opening gates and as Victoria looked behind her to see them closing, she felt a hand on her left cheek. Her head turned towards Janice, whose head was close to her now and she could see that Janice was positioning herself in for a kiss. Even at this short distance, Victoria was pleased that Janice had not recognised her. For someone who loved her young women, she had not noticed the woman whom she had ogled over for the entire session of choosing her bedroom.

Victoria pulled back "She we wait until we get inside? I don't want that perv looking in his rear view mirror at us."

"What makes you think that he won't be looking at us inside?" Janice replied.

"Because I will leave if he does. I don't do men."

"Relax, I am joking. If you want to wait, that's fine. Would you like a drink first or go straight to one of my rooms?"

"The room sounds fantastic, can we go in your biggest room?"

"Why of course" Janice answered delightfully.

They exited the car once it had entered into the courtyard which was positioned in the middle of the mansion. Four walls full of rooms and corridors surrounding the centre piece courtyard with a drive, an elongated garden which disappeared through a narrow path to the rear of the house and a statue of Venus with water protruding from her nether regions.

Janice led Victoria by the hand inside of the house. "What is your name?" she asked "Kirsty" Victoria replied.

....

"I have finally finished at the warehouse boss" Atkinson told Wallis as he sat in his car exhausted of having to summon a court order to obtain the list of bedrooms from the warehouse manager. Wallace had already come up short at the shop as she had somehow managed to delete all of her orders remotely. Wallace had instead gone to help Wallis' team until Atkinson had obtained the list. "About fucking time" Wallis replied "I can't believe that he wouldn't give us it even though she was a killer and killed those who they made the bedrooms for."

"That is unless he is working with her boss."

"Could be, I'll put a tail on him just in case. And even if he isn't, it'll serve the fucker right not being able to go somewhere without us watching him. It'll stop his affair in it's tracks straight away."

"Is he having an affair?"

"How do I fucking know, I was just quipping." and Wallis tutted to himself. "Get the first name on that list and go and investigate it now. Give me the next name and I will forward it on to Wallace."

"Tell Wallace to go to Mr Kenneth Holmes, 32 Wiltshire Road (who was actually the first person on the list) and I will investigate Ms Janice Wilton boss."

"That's right, you take the female case" Wallis laughed to him.

"Damn right. After the day I have had boss, I need to be authoritative in front of a Ms. You never knew, I might just get lucky."

Chapter 31

Victoria was led up the winding stairs, right to the top. Looking down nearly gave her vertigo but she managed to compose herself in time. They walked all the way down the corridor to the room at the end, Janice opened it up and it was exactly how Victoria had imagined it from the plans. It looked so expensive but obviously she knew otherwise. She had to pretend obviously that she didn't though.

"WOW, this room is amazing. It is probably bigger than my whole house put together" and she watched as Janice closed to curtains to the view that looked out onto the main road in front of the house. A car was leaving the premises.

"That's my driver leaving for the night in case you were worried if he was going to walk in here with his cock in his hand. Plus, it's nothing to write home about anyway, I know." she stated, winking at Victoria and drawing the other curtain closed.

"So are we alone then?"

"Of course. Just you, me and my guard dogs downstairs. Rottweilers patrolling the grounds around the house. Did you not see one of them?"

"No, afraid not. I was too busy looking at you." and as soon as that sentence had ended Janice grabbed hold of Victoria's shoulders and pushed herself onto her. Their tongues darted together as they kissed passionately, Joyce's hands speedily covering every inch of Victoria's body, well almost. Joyce immediately and without hesitation began removing Victoria's clothes.

"Wow, you don't believe in the slow method then?"

"Why, do you want me to take my time? The quicker we get naked, the more fun we can have all night."

"I suppose so" Victoria answered "Get your kit off." Janice did what she was told and stood in front of Victoria completely naked. She admired her forty something year old body and was slightly jealous. Her breasts were bigger than hers and still quite firm, the result of having no children she thought. She must visit the gym or have one in her house because her body was toned but not muscular and her buttocks were tight and not flabby. Victoria looked down at her body; hardly an inch of fat on her, toned body, smallish breasts and not much of a bottom but enough to notice in the skirt she had been wearing all day. They were complete opposites and even though Victoria was not gay, she was actually looking forward to what was about to happen. She had not experienced anything like this before so she had decided to enjoy herself before killing her.

Janice grabbed Victoria, still with her underwear on, lifted her up and threw her down onto her back on the bed. Janice parted Victoria's legs, looked between them and licked her lips. She positioned herself at the foot of the bed and slowly began to kiss each side of Victoria's legs, working herself up the bed kissing each inside leg alternatively. As she placed a hand on each side of Victoria's inner thigh Janice's mobile phone began to ring. Victoria could feel Janice's sigh through her underwear and gasped slightly in anticipation.

"Sorry" Janice said "but I am going to have to get this. My business comes first."

'Yeah before me obviously' Victoria said to herself, laughing at the prospect of it even happening. Janice answered the phone and her demeanour changed instantaneously.

Janice's replies to the other person were "Yes, no, just me and a friend, yes I am safe I have Rottweilers on my property, yes of course and I shall see you soon."

Before Janice could turn back around, Victoria had removed her bra concealing her favourite weapon and she was spinning off the bed, slicing Janice's neck with it and she was in mid air. The blood surged from her carotid artery, leaving her body in beautifully patterned interludes. She had no time to waist so as Janice's body was falling to the floor, she swept her legs ensuring she would land a her back and sliced her femoral artery as she did. Blood trickled out of that wound, obviously showing Victoria how much blood had already been lost. The look on Janice's face said it all, she was evidently face to face with the person she had just been told about.

"I am sorry it had to end like this" Victoria explained "I was actually about to enjoy being with you if it hadn't have been for your phone call." Janice's eyes just glared at her in shock. "You would have died a happy woman, not like this" and the glare became glazed as Janice died in front of her.

Victoria stood in only her knickers over Janice's body, looked down at herself covered in blood and remembered that there was an en suite attached to her bedroom. Removing her knickers quickly, she estimated that she had at least a few minutes to wash the blood from her body, get changed and get out of the grounds before whoever it was turned up.

As she exited the bathroom and back into the bedroom; not being bothered how much evidence she now left that she had been there, she quickly got changed whilst staring at Janice's now ashen body. Once all of he clothes were on, she looked back at her handy work, pulled the list out of her pocket and decided who was going to be next now she had a few more nights to kill, so to speak.

Walking down the stairs, which was still just as nauseating, she heard movement from down one of the corridors. She readied herself, removed her shoes and walked as quietly as she could. Unfortunately for her, taking her shoes off didn't make the slightest difference when she was met around the corner by a Rottweiler growling at her.

Victoria could see its hind legs about to push itself towards her, so instead of running she screamed at it at loud and as angry as she could. It almost looked shocked as it ceased growling at her and actually took a few steps back. Those steps back was all that she needed to run and towards the nearest door she could she.

As she began running, she could hear the dogs claws following her in the tiled floor, gradually drawing nearer. Victoria saw the door in sight and prayed that it was unlocked. Reaching out for the handle appeared to happen in slow motion as she saw it turn and the noise of it opening was music to her eyes like the finale of a great composition. As she exited the building, her outreaching leg kicked the door closed behind her which was followed by a loud thud on the other side of it. She was not bothered if the dog had been injured, knocked itself out or was even dead; all she did was look forward and for an escape route.

The car she entered the premises was parked just down the drive, facing the way out. Her feet pressed against the crushed slate underneath her, slightly uncomfortable but more comfortable than it would have been in her heels. The closer she got to the car, the more aware she became of dogs looking at her from various parts of the house. Fortunately all of them appeared to be inside and not outside and Janice had told her and the person on the phone.

Victoria tried the door in the vain hope that it would be open, I mean why wouldn't it when the house is protected by dogs. It was and the keys were in the ignition too. Victoria shook her head as she sat down in the driver's seat, noticing that there was a fob holder with a sticker saying Gate on it. She had really fell on her feet as she had hoped she would and pressed the button. She could hear the rattling of the gate opening in the distance and turned the key in the ignition.

Victoria put the car into gear and released the hand brake, the biting point of the car was difficult in a new car and she finally managed to achieve forward motion. She approached the end of the drive when another set of headlights beamed back at her. The car beeped its horn and flashed its lights at her and as Victoria looked closer she could see Detective Atkinson waving at her to reverse her car back into the grounds. She shook her hair and ushered for him to drive back instead which made him get out of the car and walk towards her.

Winding the window down she heard him talking to her, she didn't know how long he had been talking but she got the gist of it ".....have to move backwards as I am a Detective here to see Ms Wilton, okay?" Knowing that he had not recognised her, she reluctantly reversed the car with just enough room for him to pass her and she started to drive towards the gate again. However, in this time the gates had began to close. Victoria pressed the fob again but the gates continued to close. You must have to wait for them to fully close before they will open again.

Atkinson had noticed what was going on at this point and was currently tapping on the driver's window for her to get out of the car. His suspicion will have increased now that she had attempted to drive away.

As she got out of the car, he stared right at her and she realised that he still had no idea who she was. This was one of the lead investigators and he didn't even know it was her. "What do you think you are doing?"

"She sent me away in the middle of sex because of a phone call, I am pissed off and still horny. Wouldn't you want to leave as soon as possible?"

"I do apologise but I am going to have to ask you come back inside with me."

"Oh really, that won't be at all awkward will it now?"

"Why?"

"Because I left whilst she was in the shower."

"Oh I see, but I am still gonna need you to come inside with me. Okay?" Victoria shrugged her shoulders and nodded, looking down at the floor pretending to be embarrassed. "Which way do we go in?"

"Follow me" and Victoria led him to the door where she had left the house from. She opened the door fast and looked a bit silly as she had expected a Rottweiler to jump out at him, but it had not. It wasn't even laid prone behind the door. "The door was stiff when I left the house" she explained, and invited him to walk in before him which he declined "Show me the way please" and she led him down the corridor towards the stairs. As they entered the lobby where the stairs were, Victoria noticed a pedestal that she had not before. It had a vase sat on the top of it that looked expensive. As she walked by it, she purposely knocked into it as she turned around. It smashed onto the floor "Oh shit, sorry. I can't remember which way to go upstairs but she probably heard the smash and will be on her way now."

Victoria knelt on the floor and began collecting pieces of the vase and Atkinson joined her. As soon as he crouched down in the squatting position, she kicked her heel into the back of his neck causing his face to plant against the tiled flooring.

Grabbing a piece of the vase, she leaned over his writhing body and knicked the artery in his neck with the broken vase. While her knees were behind him, she slammed her right one into the back of his head, causing his nose to burst open on to the floor. Before he could try and even think about getting up Victoria looked around and got hold of another pillar, raised it above her head and smashed it down into his legs repeatedly.

Hearing him scream in pain let her know that the cut to his artery had not been severe enough. As she looked she could see him holding the wound, so the pillar came crashing down onto his arm that was stopping the blood flowing too. The cracks of his bones were only sparing her on even more. Atkinson laid flat, face down on the floor again, she needed to stop him moving so the pillar came down hard in the base of his neck and used like a baseball bat up and down his back until his legs stopped moving.

A different noise stopped her in her tracks, the noise was a collection of growls.

She hesitantly began to raise her head and looked around her. There must have been half a dozen Rottweilers surrounding them, all looking in their direction. Acting quickly Victoria began to walk away slowly and towards the front door at the other end of the corridor. At first the dog's heads followed her but they quickly turned their attention to Atkinson.

As Victoria stepped slowly walking backwards, facing the dogs at all times, she watched as the pack converged on Detective Atkinson and began tearing his body to shreds. There was no sound coming from him that she could hear, but the dogs were making enough noise on their own.

She continued to walk backwards until she felt the front door behind her. The handle turned and the door opened behind her, it was only then that she eventually dropped the pillar onto the floor. Upon closing the door she walked gingerly back to the car, pressed the button for the gates to open and drove out of the grounds not looking back once.

He walked out from the bushes that surrounded the house, looked over at Atkinson's car parked on the drive, looked back at Victoria leaving and decided to investigate the house for himself.

Chapter 32

Atkinson's mobile phone was vibrating in the vicinity of what was left of him when the chauffeur arrived for work the next morning.

The chauffeur shooed the two dogs that were still gnawing of his body with the weapon he had to control them, like a sort of cattle prod device but for big dogs instead. The chauffeur walked past Atkinson, ignoring the mangled body and walked up the spiral staircase towards Janice's bedroom.

As he gingerly opened the door and saw her deceased naked body laid on the floor next to her bed. As he walked closer he could see where she had been sliced open and her mobile phone was on the floor next to her too, but hers wasn't vibrating. Looking closer at her prone naked body, he noticed that the name 'Liam' had been sliced into her right breast.

He had three things he could do.

Firstly would be to call the Police straight away.

Secondly would be to hide Atkinson's body, clean up and ring the Police.

Thirdly would be to steal the hidden money he knew Janice had stashed around the house in various safes, call the Police anonymously and get the hell out of there.

Carrying the suitcases down the staircase was tough but it was a sacrifice he was willing to make to be an instant millionaire from the cash inside of them. He looked at Atkinson's corpse, now surrounded by the odd fly here and there. The phone began to vibrate again. The chauffeur picked up the phone, answered it and left it on the floor next to Atkinson. He could hear someone saying "Hello" and a few other words he couldn't make out. Phone records and GPS would be able to figure out where whoever this person was in no time.

The chauffeur picked up the bags again and exited the side of the house, immediately noticing that the car he had parked last night was now not where it should be. Without even bothering to think where it was, he opened the garage, put the suitcases into Janice's other car (one that she only went out in on special occasions), got inside and drove away.

Seven minutes later almost the whole Police force turned up at Janice's house.

The front, back and side doors were burst open within seconds of each other with dozens of Officers lining the corridors shouting, warning and telling anyone that could hear them to make themselves visible to them. The Officers at the rear found the room with the Rottweilers in. Upon noticing that nearly of them were blood stained, coupled with the fact that they ran towards them as soon as they were seen resulted in each of them being shot dead instantaneously.

The Officers from the front and the side entrances met one another at the spiral staircase were Atkinson's body was. A few of the Officers either threw up or vomited in their mouths and managed to swallow it to prevent the embarrassment. Of the lead Officers radioed for Wallace and Wallis to let them know what they had found. They could not enter until the upstairs of the building was secure. The sight of a couple of dozen Police

Officers all running up the staircase would have made a great Escher piece of artwork. They secured the upstairs with the only person found was of course Janice's dead body.

Wallace and Wallis walked up to Atkinson's mauled body and both of them wept.

Grief was quickly replaced with anger and anger was replaced with revenge.

"Get Joyce in here" Wallis shouted into his radio "I want this whole fucking place scouring for evidence." He put his radio down and turned to Wallace. "I want as much fucking evidence to point in her direction that the judge will extradite her to Texas to give her the fucking death penalty."

"Yes boss. I think we should send people to each and every name on that list who is left" Wallace recommended "What do you think?"

"Do it. We will either stop her killing people she has ear marked, catch her in the act, force her to kill unprepared or push her away." Wallis ushered Wallace away to get it done now, who left the room shouting for the Officers to follow him.

At the bottom of the stairs, Joyce was knelt next to Atkinson's body completely torn up. She turned to look at Wallace "You fucking kill that bitch Tom. You find her and kill her for doing this to Nick." and she walked towards Wallace and whispered into his ear "I will make the evidence look like you did it in revenge, just kill her. Understand?" Wallace looked deep into her eyes, there was no sarcasm, light hearted bollocks about her today. He knew that she meant every word she had said. He nodded and left the house via the side entrance, with the remainder of the Officers to brief them on the next part of the investigation.

Joyce leaned over Atkinson and zipped up the body bag, his face still partly visible. As the zip brushed past his lips, Joyce could feel the emotion of revenge bubble up even more inside of her.

Wallace had divided the Officers into ten teams, as that is how many people were left on the list. He had checked on the old man last night and he was away for a couple of weeks according to his neighbour.

All ten teams separated immediately and made their way to their assigned houses.

Chapter 33

Victoria pulled up outside of the last person on the list's house. It was 11.38pm and she was in Janice's car. She figured that she really didn't have much chance of being inconspicuous now so why not just leave the car right outside. Exiting the car she noticed that the street was deathly silent. Not a single person or pet roaming the streets. Judith's car was sat on the drive.

Judith was a lovely person, the type of person who would do anything for anybody, even if it meant putting herself out. People prayed on this part of her personality and she was often taken advantage of until she snapped, that is what had happened to her marriage.

Her husband had often come home bragging that he had been snogging, feeling up or had even shagged a local tart around the back of the local pub. He was indeed at top class wanker, she would sooner not know. They both knew that she would stay with him because of the kids, they were more important than either of them loving each other or not. Plus she was just over five foot and he was just under six foot and a big bloke. She would have no chance if she had reacted when he told of his exploits.

Finally the day had come when both of her twin daughters were leaving to go to University. Her efforts as a Mother has come to fruition as one of daughters was going on the study medicine and the other law.

As soon as they had returned home from taking them to campus, Judith had walked slowly upstairs, packed her husband's clothes into bags, left them outside of the house while he was out at the local, soaked them and waited near the front window to see him staggering home.

When he was close enough, she stood over the bags with a gas lighter and dropped it onto the bags. The bags lit up, with it being soaking in turpentine all evening. She had even thrown in a couple of canisters of deodorant in the bags, which exploded just as he approached them and the front door had closed and locked behind her.

As he picked himself up from the floor at the shock of the explosions coming from the bag, he made his way to the front door only to be met by both of Judith's older brothers with their arms crossed and shaking their heads.

From that day on, the only day she had seen him had been in court to finalise the divorce.

However tonight he had found out where she lived and was currently pinning her down on her bed, holding both arms above her as he rubbed his groin against hers, begging for her to scream so he could pummel her face into the pillow.

Victoria of course knew nothing about what she was about to walk in on as she shimmied through the open dining room window. She had changed into her kill suit in the back of Janice's car retrieving her bag from behind the drivers seat where she had left it earlier in the night. As she sneaked towards the stairs, SHE could hear talking coming from upstairs. Victoria knew that Judith was single and had never brought a man to her house when she had watched her. Either tonight was the exception or she was watching the TV in her room.

Her feet were as silent as usual scaling each step after the next. Once outside of the room she could see someone on top of Judith, both of them were dressed, he was muttering to her and grinding his pelvis onto her. Instead of bounding into the room, she walked into the room next to it and placed her ear on the wall. The wall of plaster board, installed by the bedroom fitters when they had split the main bedroom in a bedroom and a study room next to it.

Victoria stopped breathing in order to hear exactly what was happening. In the absence of all other sound, she could hear the threats he was making towards her. She heard him telling her how he was about to make her pay for not allowing him to see his own daughters, followed by the fact that he had sexually abused them from them being eleven years old up to the point of them leaving to go to University.

As soon as that left his lips, Victoria could hear Judith thrashing about the bed calling him all the evil cunts under the sun through her grinding teeth. When she had finished swearing at him and spitting in his face, he told her that he was going to rape her soon and there was nothing she could do about it. With that he heard a strike and muffling, Victoria surmised that he had hit her and stuffed something into her mouth. She heard a lot of scuffling and movement from the creaked of the bed.

Turning around in the room, she looked for anything that would help her finish this kill and get the fuck out as soon as possible. She had not planned for a six foot man being here too. It was hard to see things in the dark room but spotted something after a little while.

As Victoria laid on the floor flat at the base of the bedroom door, she waited to see his naked body perched above Judith's and about to violate her. It was then that she began to slowly and gradually push the bedroom door open centimetre by centimetre.

Shimmying across the bedroom floor with a handful of knitting needles wasn't the most comfortable or quite thing she had ever done. Thankfully (for her) the other two people in the rooms were too preoccupied with what was happening to even notice.

Victoria knelt up behind his massive frame and waited for the opportunity to arise. As his arse gyrated in front of her until she had positioned herself exactly. When the moment was right she slammed one of the needles into and up his arsehole as hard as she could. His body clenched immediately but as she jumped up, her foot kicked the needle another few inches inside of him, causing his body to fall backwards. As she landed with both feet on top of the mattress she jumped onto his chest, pulling two other needles out of her cleavage and was now pushing each one into his eye sockets. He fell onto another one she had positioned sticking up at the end of the bed which pushed upward through his throat as she push the ones into his eye sockets. She was now standing on his shoulders with his legs bent double underneath him with four needles inside of his body and screaming in agony. Her weapon came out and sliced his neck severing his vocal chords, she loved doing that. As she wrote Liam's name into his stomach, Victoria was aware of movement behind her and saw Judith running past her and towards the bedroom door.

"STOP!" Victoria shouted. This was the first time she had talked to one of her victims whom she had not incapacitated first. Judith stopped dead in her tracks. "You have no fear, now I have killed him I will be on my way. I will leave you in peace for you to tell the Police what happened here."

Judith turned around and stared right into Victoria's eyes. "They will believe you as I have left my calling card on this waste of spunk's stomach." Judith walked towards her ex husband's body and pushed the needles right into his head so only the nubs at the end were poking out of them. Judith flung her arms around Victoria and began to sob. She cried loud and for longer than anyone had ever been close to Victoria without them either ending up dead or the thought at least entering her head.

Victoria looked into Judith's eyes as their bodies parted, her face was grimaced for a few seconds and she looked down at her body. Her hands felt around her abdomen wear Victoria's weapon had pierced it and was now gushing blood from the wound. "Shit woman" Victoria shouted "I was gonna let you go to tell the story." Looking down at the wound and the blood on Judith's hands and now feet where it had dripped, she knew what had to happen. "Why did you have to take me by surprise and leap onto me? You have wounded yourself and won't survive before help arrives. I will have to make it quick for you honey."

Victoria walked up to Judith and plunged the weapon deep into her heart and pulled it out, guiding her body onto the floor as she withdrew it. Turning around, she looked at her work. Her improvisational skills at this was getting better and more honed. Maybe she could fit another couple in tonight before they find Atkinson at Janice's house.

Victoria walked out of Judith's house covered in blood on her kill suit, got into the car, looked at the list and picked the fifth one down.

His head popped up from behind his steering wheel, turned the ignition and drove after her keeping his lights off to begin with so she would not see him.

Chapter 34

It was now 1.18am and Victoria was about to perform her fifth kill of the night. She was including Atkinson as hers as he would have died whether the dogs turned up or not.

Tony was a geek, plain and simple. Now there is nothing wrong with being a geek and he was a massive one. He knew when every new game was coming out for each console, what the pre sale reviews said about them and how long it would probably take to complete it. He loved all the Sci-fi genre of films, books and conventions. The conventions was the closest he got to almost naked women in his packed calendar. His parents were high flyers in their professions, funding his lifestyle and buying his house and car for him. He had not worked a single minute in his life, unless you call reviewing games and it appearing in magazines constitutes as a job.

Most of his day and night consisted of him either being on his consoles, laptop, tablet or talking about them with similar like minded geeks at a local coffee shop. He had never actually had the chance to touch a female intimately or even seen a fully naked one in person. His browser history was empty of such material, he was pure and simply only interested in games, films and TV programmes. His love for The Big Bang Theory was beyond being a huge fan. It gave him the hope that he too could emulate being one of them one day.

Today had been no different to any of the past forty seven he had. Playing the latest role playing game online with his online mates until midnight ish until his eyes could not take any more and he had tucked himself up into his Star Trek duvet set. He always slept with the window open as living alone was still a bit creepy for him to get over. He wanted to be able to hear anyone trying to break into his car or walking up the gravel drive if they were going to try and break into his house. He had an alarm that you could even set for the sensors downstairs to be left on whilst you were upstairs which he not only used during the night but also when he was on his games with his headphones plugged in.

Victoria pulled up outside of Tony's house and noticed the flashing light on the front attached to a big white box. Victoria knew that this one is always used as a decoy box and the one on the rear of the house is the real one. She had been here before but never inside of the house. The gravel drive was easy to get around by her just walking on next door's drive and scaling the fence into Tony's back garden. Victoria shimmied up the drainpipe and onto the flat roof, fitting through the gap in the back bedroom window that Tony probably thought no-one could get through was a mistake.

Once in the house, she remained perfectly still until she knew that he was asleep or transfixed on one of his games. Her ploy to lure him in was simple, it was the same way she had managed to get Janice interested. Her kill suit dropped to the floor and she stood there in her underwear. Stepping out of the suit smudged a little bit of Judith's blood into the carpet, still not dried completely on her suit. As Victoria left the back bedroom she listened as to which room Tony was in and the noises led her to the left and in the far room on the right. The door opened gradually and she could see him wrapped up in his duvet that his parents had more than likely bought him while he was still at him.

Stood at the end of the bed, she coughed which awoke him suddenly from his slumber. Tony sat bolt upright in bed and stared at Victoria in her underwear.

"Whoa" rubbing his eyes "What is going on? Who, who are you?" Victoria stood perfectly still and said nothing. Instead she crouch slightly and removed her knickers and threw them out of the door into the corridor.

"What do you want?" and Victoria stretched her arm out in front of her and with her forefinger, pointed straight at Tony. Her arm turned over and the forefinger was now ushering him towards her.

Like someone in a transfixed state, he began to move closer and closer to her. His duvet peeling back over his body to reveal his upper torso naked and an erection in his Green Arrow underpants, quite appropriate really. Victoria looked down at his erection and motioned for him to remove his underwear.

Standing up on the mattress he slowly and almost reluctantly but really wanting to, pulled his underwear over his swollen appendage and it sprang over the waistband. Again Victoria ushered Tony closer to her and he began to walk down the bottom of the bed. "Did Mark send you?" he asked "I bet this is the gift he sent me after he lost his bet. Do I have to pay you afterwards?" she shook her head so he positioned his erection close to Victoria's mouth with him standing on the bed and her on the floor. All of a sudden he was becoming more confident once he thought that a mate had paid her to come to him and rid him of his virginity.

"Are you going to take that off now?" as he pointed to her bra "They aren't really big are they but they will do I suppose." Victoria reached around her back and as she did, he erection touched the tip of her lips. She hooked her bra and allowed it to fall to the floor.

As her hands moved to the front of her body, all Tony was looking at was the position of her mouth near his erection. The reflection of the light on her weapon was far too in his peripheral vision to see until his cock fell to the floor and blood spurting onto his wardrobe behind her after she had dodged out of the way once the slice had removed it from his body. In the milliseconds that followed Tony stood both in excruciating pain, shock and disbelief that his cock was actually no longer attached to his body. His legs buckled underneath him and as his body followed, Victoria wrapped her legs around his neck and snapped it after a few tugs backwards.

Liam's name was carved into Tony's neck, she put her clothes back on and walked towards his bedroom window which looked out onto the street. As she pulled the curtains back, she noticed someone crouched behind Janice's car. The shadow of them crouched down could be seen at the rear of the car and Victoria stood mesmerised at the shadow not moving at all for a full five or so minutes.

Suddenly the person stood up slightly, looking over the roof of the car finding themselves staring at Victoria looking out of the window right at them. She could see that it was a man's build but she couldn't see his face and he had a hoodie on obscuring the shape of his head. Like a flash of lightening, Victoria sped out of the bedroom, down the stairs setting the alarm off, turned the key in the door and ran outside to her car.

With the house alarm blurting out at full throttle she stood on the road looking around but she could not see a sole anywhere. No-one was even visibly looking out of their curtains in the neighbourly way, to check if anyone was breaking into the house. When she was sure that the person was no longer in the vicinity or hiding in the back of the car, she sped back into the house and removed the fuse from the alarm, silencing it.

Victoria walked back to Janice's car, turned the ignition and drove away to the nearest safe place to park to try and get around her head if she actually saw the person that she did. She knows that she did but questioning herself was the only way she could get around what just happened in her head.

Who would be crouched behind her car? The Police? No, they would have been there in force and would have arrested her by now.

A car thief was the most logical explanation and the one that her mind finally settled on. She really shouldn't have though, as it had been the person who had been watching what she was doing for a very long time now. He had been there after every one of her kill that she had planned from a bedroom she had designed. And now he was following her on her current tirade of murder.

She worked out in her head that she could fit in at least another two kills before it got light. After those she would have to go into hiding, completely change her appearance or move to another part of the country or world.

Looking down the list Victoria looked at number seven, lucky number seven. Thinking about it, she should have rid the world of this person before Janice, Judith or Tony but the times were not right at the time.

Patricia worked nights and would not be ready for until she got home from work. Working it out, Victoria knew that she would have a few hours inside of one of the hiding places before she got home and more used to what she was used to doing, instead of improvising.

Chapter 35

Victoria had already been in place for a good two hundred and seventy seven minutes before she heard the car pull up on the drive. According to her watch, Patricia was a little late home from work than she usually was.

She had pulled up outside of her house at 4.23am, searched the vicinity as this neighbourhood is quite active with burglars and drug dealers/takers on some nights and walked around the back of the house. The flimsy and quite shoddy frame of the back porch was embarrassingly easy to penetrate. Once she had gained access to that, the spare key under the upturned bucket on the right of the step was most helpful to aid her cause.

Knowing that she had full reign of the house for at least a few hours she made herself a drink and something to eat. She had not had anything for almost two days now and she was beginning to feel it.

When she was suitably refreshed and full up she assumed her position in her hiding place after admiring the great work that the fitters had done to make it exactly how she had planned it to look. As usual she knew that she would be there for a while so she planned out in her head where everything was that she had seen in the house, how she was going to kill Patricia and how she would make her escape and likely move to another part of the country with a different name.

After sorting it all out in her head what she would do and how she would do it, she laid there awaiting her next victim. Although she was a couple of minutes later than she usually was. It was then that she heard the car pull up onto the drive.

....

Wallace's team and the other nine converged on their selected houses. There was no plan of smashing into the houses at exactly the same time, just when they got there and the tactical leader of each team decided that it was time. Wallis just wanted all of the people safe and hopefully find Victoria in the act if they were lucky.

They had all set off from Janice's house at 6.03am.

At 6.22am the first team made contact with the rest that Tony Classis' dead body had been found with his penis removed from his body and Liam's name carved into his neck. The remaining nine teams suddenly became more nervous and enthralled at the outcome of their search.

At 6.43am the second team has reported that Judith Carey's dead body as well as another dead male in the house had been found with Liam's name cut into the male's stomach. Again this made the other eight teams even more alert that she had already been to two other houses and the likelihood or them either finding a dead body or her was becoming more of a possibility.

Wallace ordered his team to wait for a few minutes surrounding their house first, with the three Officers at the rear of the property to be the first to gain access into the house. All of a sudden a car was indicating to pull into the drive, Wallace leaped from behind a parked van and stopped her from doing so. She wound down her window but he put his finger up to his mouth to tell her to be quite. Wallace whispered to her what was going on and on his signal she would drive up on the drive and the Officers would enter the house a few seconds afterwards. Even though Patricia was now shitting herself, she did what Wallace told her to do; handing his men her house keys once she had closed her car door.

The Officers opened the door with the key to make it sound as normal as possible and they all converged on the bedrooms at once. Their eyes darting over each and every bit of the bedrooms just like they had been trained, checking every cupboard and wardrobe, every loose floorboard or odd sounding bit of a wall. The Officers searched the whole upper floor and found no-one. Wallace ordered the three officers at the rear of the property to gain entry. They immediately noticed that the porch had been broken into and the back door was still open with the key inside of it. This was reported back to Wallace. The Officers searched the whole of the downstairs, again using each skill that they had in a vain attempt to find Victoria but came up with a blank. This was also reported to Wallace, who was stood outside with Patricia. Wallace told the team to leave the house and handed Patricia off to one of the Officers, walking into the house himself.

Wallace walked straight up the stairs, totally discounting that she may be hiding in the lower part of the house for a change, entered the main bedroom, looked directly at the wardrobe and spoke.

"I know that you are in here Victoria" he began. "And do you know how I know that you are in here? I will tell you. I am the one who you saw staring at you outside of Tony's house four hours ago. I am the one who has been following you this whole time. I am the one who has been watching you watching them. I am the one who wants to join you on your quest to make this a better world. I understand where you are coming from and I want to help you."

Wallace listened for a reply, a movement or anything. "You probably think that this is a Police set up, but if it were I could have arrested you right after you killed Peggy the first time couldn't I? Think about it."

The mention of Peggy Glanton, the eight seven year old who was Victoria's first kill gave her a shiver all of the way down her spine but she managed to remain perfectly still.

"Anyway, if you want to talk to me about any of them and how I know what I do; I suggest that you meet me at the Humber Bridge Country Park where you killed that runner. I will be there at ten o'clock tonight. There are plenty of places for you to hide and make sure that I come alone." Wallace took a deep breath before he uttered the next words. "However, if you fail to turn up I will visit every member of your family and do the same to them as you have done to your victims. Knock once to tell me this is all clear to you" and he listened.

No knock came. "Okay do it your way" and Wallace began to walk out of the bedroom."

Victoria knocked from her hiding place. Wallace stopped in his tracks, smiled wryly "Thank you Victoria, see you later, by the ponds."

She waited until she new she was alone in the upstairs of the house before relaxing her body, putting her hands on her temples and tried to make sense of all of this. She needed a plan, the best plan that she had ever come up with and it had to be full proof.

Chapter 36

For six hours Victoria waited, waiting for the Officers to finally disappear. Knowing that Wallace had more than likely asked them to stay longer than they should just so she couldn't leave and prepare fully for tonight, she decided to plan everything from her hiding space instead.

At 1.34pm Victoria heard Patricia step back into her house talking to someone. The person she was talking to was probably a trainee Officer who had been assigned to make her feel better in her house. They wouldn't be staying in the house, they usually waited outside the front door or at the top of a drive, alternating every few hours between trainees.

Patricia's footsteps slowly and anxiously making their way up the stairs and entering the bedroom alone told Victoria something. This was obviously a message from Wallace, Patricia was the sacrificial lamb being led to the slaughter to show how much he really does want to join her. She and possibly the Officer were to show Victoria that he is indeed serious and that he will tread a thin line himself in order for the cause.

There was one thing that kept ringing around her head however. If they did indeed meet and both agreed to work together, how the hell could she get away with what she had already done now that the whole Police force knew who she was. I mean yes, he is a

Detective and will know some people that could change everything about her, but surely the line had been crossed now had it not?

The sound of the curtains closing snapped Victoria from her train of thought followed by Patricia getting undressed and rooting around her chest of drawers for everything she needed to at least try and get some sleep. The tot of rum that the Officer had suggested was already beginning to take effect and together with the strong painkillers she had in a cupboard in the bathroom would at least ensure a few hours if she could turn her brain off at least.

Victoria knew that Patricia used ear plugs to drown out the sound of the 'day people' making far too much noise for her to sleep and that she occasionally wore a face mask to prevent the daylight from penetrating her eye lids, keeping her awake. She suspected that both of these factors would be in place if she really needed to get to sleep, so as she began to move from her hiding place she knew that at least she had a little amount of leeway regarding noise. Now Victoria was always deathly silent but with the revelation of that Wallace had given her, her mind was in a dozen different places.

Even though her mind usually transfixed in the matter in hand when she was about to rid the world of another waste of energy, this time just couldn't help but being different. The thought of him being at every single one of her kills was beginning to haunt her imagination and it was something that she was extremely uncomfortable with.

As she stood up from her crouch, retrieving what she needed from what she lad left in her bag that was again hidden at the foot of the bed, now stood looking over Patricia's body. For a moment Patricia didn't look like Patricia; this made Victoria stop in her tracks, enhance her hearing for a set up and people surrounding her. For that moment she thought that the woman laid in the bed was in fact an Officer and the moment she touched her the whole force would converge on her.

Standing as still as she could at the foot of the bed weighing up whether that was Patricia or not was wasting time. It was either now or never, so she reached underneath the covers being careful not to disturb Patricia's slumber and slowly injected her just below the ankle and waited. At the moment of the injection, Patricia jerked in the bed possibly assuming that she had been bitten. Her left hand had reached down to swat or squash whatever it was that had and she felt the blood that had trickled out of the puncture would she had given herself with Victoria having to, at light speed, remove the needle.

She sat up in bed, removed the mask and looked at her hand that now had a smear of blood of it. The sight of the blood appeared to freak her out as she jumped up onto her knees and began to make her way down the bed on them. It wasn't until she reached the foot of the bed that the chemicals began to work causing Patricia's upper body to slam off the foot of the bed and directly onto the carpeted floor.

As Patricia lay there, completely unable to move with her upper torso face down on the floor but her lower torso still hanging diagonally onto the foot of the bed with her legs just above her knees still laid on the bed, she saw two feet walk around the other side of the bed and make their way right in front of her face. All attempts to move, scream or do anything had failed. She was muscularly paralysed but still had full insight as to what was happening, apart from the ear plugs muffling every movement.

The sudden pain from the back of her head as Patricia felt herself being dragged up by her hair was, she thought, the worst pain she had ever felt. As her vision rose, she could now see who this person was that had paralysed her. She could not believe that the slight woman in black in front of her was the one responsible for it and was looking around the room with just her eyes for an accomplice.

"What are you looking at?"Victoria whispered "That Officer down there is not here to help you, in fact he will be next thanks to you. Just think of that, it is your fault his family are gonna be grieving for him in a few hours. Anyway, you don't deserve an explanation and I certainly don't have the time to fuck about with you so now you are going to die, just so you know." Patricia of course could only her mumbles through the ear plugs but managed to lip read the 'going to die' part of the conversation.

Patricia's eyes began to fill with tears, which was the only response she could muster. Behind the tears she could see Victoria approaching her and beginning to tear the vest off that she was wearing for bed. Out of nowhere a blade appeared in her field of vision and she was forced to watch as Victoria wrote something across her breasts. She could just make out that it was the name Liam. As soon as the recognition of his name entered her head everything else became dark as Victoria replaced her mask and the stinging sensations from the top of her thighs began. After a minute or so Patricia could feel herself becoming increasingly sleepy and the last thing she heard was the loud banging on her bedroom window as she passed away.

The trainee Officer burst through the front door and up the stairs after hearing the prolonged banging on the front bedroom window. Unfortunately he was in so much of a rush, he slammed against the closed bedroom door flinging it open to reveal Patricia's dead body with Liam's name carved into her breasts and numerous wounds on her thighs were the arteries had obviously been severed. It was too late to think anything else as Victoria came from behind the door and sliced his neck from one side to the other causing him to slump to his knees, clutching his neck as if to push the blood back into his body.

Victoria walked to the front of the Officer got her palm ready and thrust it as hard as her could into the bridge of his nose, instantly knocking him out.

Once Victoria had admired her work, she perused Patricia's wardrobe for clothes. She was only one or two sizes above her so she was sure she could find something to fit her that would enable her to leave and roam the streets until she found another car to take her to the Humber Bridge at least.

Butterflies entered her stomach for the first time in a long while. She still didn't know whether he really wanted to work with her and if he did, whether she wanted to work with him. One thing was for sure, she wanted to know what he knew about her first.

Chapter 37

She watched from afar waiting for Wallace to arrive and to see if he brought any company. They were due to meet at ten o'clock and she had been here at seven forty-two, as soon as dusk had set in. From visiting this place before she had killed Damien, she knew the best place to position herself in order to be able to see him arrive.

Checking her watch, ten o'clock had arrived and passed by. She gave him until ten fifty and decided to leave, she knew that she may have been set up, fully expecting every exit to now be blocked by Police Officers with any attempt to leave being thwarted. She stepped down from her vantage point and as soon as her feet touched the ground she felt a hand on her shoulder.

"I wondered how long you were going to stop up there" Wallace said, catching her forearm as it span around to connect with the side of his head. "I was here when you got here and I have been watching you waiting for me."

"How did I not see you?"

"You know that it may be possible that someone is better than you at something and you are not the best at everything Victoria."

"Piss off wanker. Why am I here then? Are you gonna take me in or finish me off?" and Wallace laughed in her face. "Neither of those things my darling. I told what I want from you, a partnership."

"I don't work with anyone else, what I do is for my own means and no-one elses" and thought about her answer. "However, in my current predicament, a partnership may be a wise decision."

"Only in your current predicament eh? You thinking of severing ties once you are done with me?" as they turned around to face each other.

"I was thinking that yes" and looked into his eyes to see what he was thinking. "Anyway before anything else happens between us, I need to know how much you know about me. Everything."

"You really want to know? You really want me to tell you everything that I know about you?"

"What do you fucking think? I am not going any further into this until you tell me."

"Well I am not staying here, there is a Premier Inn close by, why don't we go there and rent a room. I can tell you everything there."

"If you think that you are pinning me down in a hotel room, you obviously don't know me very well. My last experience in a hotel didn't work out too good for me did it?"

"I thought you did superb, ridding the world of that arsehole Hackett." Wallace took a deep breath "That jumped up self aggrandising twat thought he was better than everyone else. I have known about you since you two days after you killed those people having an affair. That is how good I am."

"Are you now? Carry on."

"Can't we do this with a drink in hand? I would prefer it that way." He could see the cogs turning in her head and he hoped that he had pricked her curiosity enough for her to agree.

"We go but on one condition, the room we get is on the ground level and I stay nearest the door at all times." Wallace smiled and agreed.

Room 219 was on the ground floor and nearest the fire exit at the bottom of the corridor. He sat on the bed and she sat on the wooden yet 'meant to be comfortable' chair at the end of the dresser near the bathroom. Both had an alcoholic drink in hand, purchased from the bar at the attached pub and taken to their room by Wallace.

Whilst he had been out of the room she had surveyed every exit strategy, positioned things around the room from her bag in case she had needed them later. She knew that he knew she would be getting herself ready in case he tried to attack her. Victoria had also made Wallace drink from both glasses in case he had spiked one of them and waited a few minutes before taking a sip for herself.

"This is comfortable isn't it?" Wallace passed comment.

"Quit the niceties shit Wallace, get on with telling me what you know."

"Firstly, if we are working together my name is Tom. I get sick of being called my surname at work, right?"

"Fine, whatever you want. Tom." emphasising the Tom with a hint of get on with it thrown in.

"Well with Jacqui and Ian, the couple having the affair, I immediately noticed the similarities from the previous three murder that Detectives Grant and Willington had been investigating. It was such a shame about Willington, as he was such a great Detective to aspire to. He once told me about a cases that were shoved in a box, in a room when there was not an immediate suspect and when Detectives retired not long afterwards who had taken the case. This such of a room pricked up my ears and in my spare time I began to sift through them all."

"Bit of a nosey bastard eh?"

"It comes with the job. Anyway, I knew that whoever had killed the previous four couples must have started somewhere, so I began to look. It took me hours and hours of cases that I could have solved with my eyes closed until I found Peggy. It was then that I began to search for who Peggy had in her life. There weren't that many people were there Victoria?"

"No there wasn't. She was a sad, lonely old woman whose family did not give a fuck about. I was one of the true friends she had."

"And you killed her?"

"Yes I did, but only at her request."

"What? Are you trying to tell me that your first kill was one of her wanting you to?"

"Peggy was a very intelligent lady. She was a smart, funny, loving and caring lady. She had made mistakes in her past but don't we all? She was ill and had no-one else apart from Jeremy Kyle to swear at every morning, the Politicians to swear at lunch time and the soaps to swear at on an evening. She hated the inept, incompetent and incoherent."

"I had no idea that you liked her. I mean, I knew that you had to visit her as part of your shop lifting penalty." Victoria smiled, the first time he had seen that in a while but he also knew why she was smiling.

"At last, finally something you admit that you don't know about me."

"So when we visited your workplace and your name popped up, I immediately knew that I had heard that name in one of the cases I had researched." Ignoring the fact that she had been right about something "My boss had already ignored my theory of this case being linked to any others and had halted me in pursuing other avenues into them, so I immediately pursued them in my own time."

"Peggy became to be a dear friend and I cried for days after I had taken her life. She promised me to make it quick, which I did. It had taken months of her pleading me, bribing me with her life savings, to take her life. It wasn't until I had visited her after a latest course of radiotherapy that I agreed to put her out of her misery. She began to tell me of different ways that she would allow me to kill her. Injected her, causing paralysis and cut her arteries with one of her kitchen knifes. It didn't take long for her to pass away. I took what was mine and never looked back."

"What made you kill the rest? How do you justify what you have done after Peggy?"

"A mixture of two emotions really. First was that of taking someone's life and having to do it again. The second was Peggy and her loathing for those people who were beneath her. And me."

"So how did you perfect your skills so well in the gap from killing Peggy to the couples?"

"I never, the couples were my warm up kills. I just guess that Peggy taught me well and that I took to it excellently as I do everything else."

"And what about Martin?" which Victoria looked quizzically at Tom at the mention of his name, then realised who he actually meant.

"Oh, he knew nothing about any of this. He didn't even know anything about Peggy or my shoplifting penalty as I had used another name which I had set up just in case my past caught up with me."

"So he is as genuine as he appears?"

"Yes he is. He is a sweet, lovely man who does not deserve any of what will happen to his business because of me. I will make it up to him one day."

"Really? How?" but Victoria just tapped her nose with her right forefinger.

What followed what a very uncomfortable pause of around half of a minute; in which they both stared at each other, looked at their drinks, the walls of the hotel and all of the furniture enclosed. "So shall I address the elephant in the room?" Victoria piped up "You want to join me then? Why?"

"You don't know what it feels like when we see people get away with things like I do. It takes so much time and energy to find someone who has done wrong, building up a case, getting everything prepared and making sure you dot the i's and cross the t's; just to see it all get pissed away because one person didn't put sugar in their tea once or something shit like that" Tom began. "It is so infuriating and quite frankly I have been sick of the whole process for far too long now."

"So what you are saying is that you want to work with me to ensure that criminals get their comeuppance and I am the person who is ridding the world of people whom I consider are beneath me?"

"Yes, well surely those criminals will be beneath you too won't they? The scum of the Earth, the drug dealers, the abusers and the vile?"

"You have been watching me for all of this time and yet you still do not understand me." Victoria took a full breath "So what happens next when I say no to you?"

"I had not thought about it to be honest", which was of course a lie. He had done nothing but think about what he could do or not do if she turned him down. "Erm........", sounding like he was making it up as he went along "we could just go our separate ways, you move away and the cases will eventually go cold and I will have to go ahead alone and risk my life for my cause. Or I could try and persuade you with the lives of your family members."

The mention of her family being hurt again did nothing but make her angry. "How the fuck do you know where or who my family members are?"

"I am in the Police force my sweetheart, how do you think?"

"You mean the same Police force that searches its own staff for what they look for? And if my family were to end up dead, they would see why you were looking in them and catch you out red handed, making you a prime suspect, finding you guilty and ending up being bummed by a big fat bloke called Maury in prison? That sort of Police force?" Again another pause filled the air.

"Don't think you can threaten me TOM, I know each and every way this could go and the only person who has the upper hand is me. So you may be a better watcher than me but I did still spot you eventually. Besides I haven't said no, I merely asked what would happen next if I said no."

"If you say yes, you would have free reign on anyone you would like but you would also have to help me too. You watch them when I can't and collaborate when they needed to be killed."

"Not much in it for me, seeing as though I could just walk away now is there?" and Victoria stood up from the chair and walked towards the door. Tom didn't move, apparently calling her bluff. However when her hand touched the door handle he sped at her, grabbed her right forearm and flung her into the dresser below the television. Her body contorted, wrapping around the cabinet like a piece of plasticine and landing heavily on the floor. Victoria grabbed her back as she suddenly felt more pain in those few seconds than she ever had done, physical pain anyway.

Tom walked meaningfully in Victoria's direction, wanting to build on his momentum to keep on top of her. He after all knew what she was capable of, and as he reached her trying to get up, he punched the right side of her face causing her to reach the floor again with high velocity. Waiting to see if she moved, which she didn't, he walked over to her bag and emptied it out of the window "What are you going to do to me without any of your fucking toys? You have made the worst decision of your life and I am going to end up being promoted, making it even easier to carry out my plan now. I really hoped that you would see sense and join me."

Victoria stirred on the ground, lifted her head up as much as she could and looked deep into Tom's eyes "Why don't you quit fucking whining like a pussy and kill me? It's better than listening to this shit." and began laughing causing the blood inside of her mouth to spit onto the hotel room floor.

Enraged at this Tom walked from the window, grasped hold of Victoria's kill suit at the top of her buttocks and the collar, lifted her up and threw her into the wall at the back of the headboard. Her body bounced off it like it had been the wall of a child's bouncy castle. Tom reached inside the front of the kill suit and began feeling around her breasts. When he couldn't find what he wanted he appeared very shocked. "Where have you hidden it? I know that is where you usually keep it."

"You really don't want to know where I have hidden it Tom" she stated, "you would love getting it from there."

"You're right I would" he exclaimed taking hold of her arms, wrapping them around her back and ripping the suit off Victoria's body until she lay there naked with random bits of her suit still clung to her body. Tom looked down at her "Are you not going to stop me?" he asked, feeling her body submit to him.

"How do you know that is exactly how I wanted this to happen?" was her reply.

He positioned his right hand between her legs as his other hand held her arms behind her back and gradually made his way to the lips of her vagina. As his finger tips touched her warm welcoming parts, her knee lifted catching Tom square under his chin causing the protruding tongue that was stuck out in the height of his concentration to almost be bitten clean off. Blood streamed out of the wound with the other third of his tongue hanging on for dear life. Now in a state of shock, Victoria sprung into life performing a kip up to find herself standing in front of Tom. Her foot connected with his testicles with such force that the pain now replaced the pain from his two thirds detached tongue. Her hands clapped as hard as they could against each ear, causing tinnitus and severe head pain again; but even in as much pain as he was he spotted her weapon tucked under the pillow which had moved from him throwing her into the wall. With all of his muster he crawled towards the pillow and reached for the object and as he turned around he felt the blade enter his heart as he was waiting for him to turn around.

Bemused he looked in his hand what he had collected. It was a syringe and with the last ounce of energy, plunged the needle into cut on Victoria's upper arm she had sustained after being flung into the cabinet, and sunk his thumb onto the depressor causing all of the liquid to enter her body.

Looking down at the weapon sticking out of his chest, he could see her pull it out and his chest felt like it was collapsing inside of itself.

As he began to lose consciousness, he saw Victoria stagger towards the window, collecting something off the floor as she did and then all was dark.

Tom Wallace died twenty seconds after this moment.

Chapter 38

Twenty seven minutes after Tom passed away, the paramedics were still working on him on the floor of the hotel room.

Everyone in the room could hear Joyce screaming at the top of her voice as a six foot black bag was placed around Victoria's body. As the sound echoed around the room of the bag being zipped up, Joyce spat on her as many times as she could whilst trying to be held back by two Officers and threatened with dismissal from Chief Inspector Wallis.

"Have you finished now?" Wallis asked Joyce with that look in his eye that she should have been more professional.

"I frankly can't believe that you are being so restrained, Sir" with the 'Sir' part emphasised emphatically. Wallis stood up from Tom's body, let go of his hand and faced her. "If you don't think that I have all of those emotions going around my body that you have in yours, then you are so wrong. However, one of my men is being worked on down here and I have already lost another one twenty four hours ago. It will be my pleasure to burn her body into ashes and spread them in an unmarked grave, but unfortunately she still may have had a loving family who will want a proper funeral for her."

"Oh come on!" Joyce sounded out.

"Yes, yes Joyce and just because you don't like it, it doesn't make it so. Now go with her while I stay with my man here. It is obvious what has happened to him, I want to know how she died. Kapeesh?" Joyce saluted to Wallis and left the room mumbling something under her breath.

Wallis' attention was drawn to Tom again. The paramedics had switched around from performing CPR (Cardio Pulmonary Resuscitation) on him as it was such a tiring thing to do. The lead paramedic turned to look at Wallis, he shook his head and they continued to work on Tom.

Joyce watched as her colleagues placed Victoria's body into the back of the van on the stretcher, shut the doors and drove away. Standing there she thought about the time she had been flirting with the supermarket owner and Victoria had been stood right behind her the whole time. All of those times Wallace, Atkinson and then Hackett had visited the shop and there had been no inkling that she was the one they were looking for. All of the time they had thought and were so sure that it was a man that they were looking for. Only a man would remove the testicles from another man unless she had a history of abuse. Only a man had the strength to overpower most of the people she had killed, unless she had uncanny power for someone of her stature. Only a man would be so evil to perform a lot of the things that had been done to the victims.

'Sexist bastards' Joyce thought, got into her car and followed the van to the station.

Another fifteen minutes followed and the lead paramedic took Wallis to aside and told him that all efforts were fruitless, Tom had not been alive when they got here and they had not been able to get a single life sign from him whilst they were working on him. Reluctantly Wallis finally allowed the paramedics to call it. Tom Wallace had died but it was definitely not for the want of them trying to bring him back.

Joyce pulled up in her usual parking space in the station's car park, walked towards the security guard who worked every weekday, winked and licked her lips at him as she always did and entered the building.

The walk to her office was one of sombre, she was pleased that no-one else was going to die but she had lost colleagues and friends in this war and that was something she was never going to be able to forget or forgive herself for. She had been right this whole time about things but it had been immediately dismissed so she had not thought any more about it. Her coat hung on the back of her chair, her bag over the coat and pushed her chair under the desk and turned her computer on. She signed onto the Police network and opened a page ready for Victoria's autopsy, saved it and sent it to the PC in the autopsy room. This was going to be the most enjoyable autopsy she had ever performed.

Joyce knew that she wouldn't feel any of it but she hoped that somewhere out there; Victoria would be watching her enjoying slicing her whole body up, separating it into different sections and then the whole lobotomy once it had been agreed, which it would do if she pushed it to be.

With all of this on her mind she forgot to collect her handbag and closed the door on it as she made her way downstairs.

Wallis sat on the end of the bed and surveyed the room from where he was. Moving up the bed backwards using his back stretched arms to propel him, he felt a pain in the palm of his hand. When he looked down at it he could see a minute speck of blood oozing from just below his thumb.

Jumping down off the bed and onto the floor, he wanted to see what had caused it. There was nothing under the bed and upon closer inspection, nothing under the mattress either so he pulled back the bed sheets and gently pressed down where he had been when he felt the puncture wound. After a few compresses of the mattress he found where it was by causing himself yet another puncture wound, this time on the palm of his other hand.

Once he had found the origin of it, he noticed that there was a rip on the material of the mattress. Pulling the material to the side he spotted the needle and once he had uncovered the whole syringe with great delicacy, he stared at it wondering what it was doing there. It couldn't be coincidence, so he bagged it up from one that he always keeps in his jacket pocket for these exact 'just in case' moments and sealed it to take to Joyce's team.

The moment the bag was in his hand and walking towards the hotel room door, the dizziness had set in and Wallis hit the floor like someone had pulled the energy chord from his body. He felt his whole body become paralysed but his mind was fully active. Once he stopped himself from going into shock he composed himself.

The first words to enter his head were *Victoria is not dead.*

Chapter 39

Victoria's body was brought into the cold room. Joyce had her back to the body staring at her computer screen as her colleagues unzipped the bag, peeled it back over Victoria's body, turned her to remove the bag and took a few pictures. They took a picture of her for every piece of the remaining pieces of her kill suit that they had removed from her body. Once they were satisfied with those pictures they turned Victoria's body over and took pictures of her face down. Again, they turned her back once they were happy with the pictures that they had taken.

Joyce turned around from her computer wearing a headset that was bluetooth linked to her autopsy programme so she could explain what she was doing and what she found as she was going along. Her colleagues, Gavin and Pete, handed her the camera and she connected it to the autopsy programme too and left the room to go through the items that they had found at the scene.

Once the pictures had uploaded, Joyce took about fifteen minutes zooming into different wounds on the pictures and walking over to Victoria's body to compare and clarify what she thought the wounds were and how she had gotten them.

Once Joyce got to the wound in her upper arm and zoomed right in, she could see that there was another wound inside of the wound. A small puncture wound like from a needle inside of it.

Needing a second opinion, she took off the headset and went into the next room to speak to Gavin, her second in command for his opinion.

The second that the door closed and locked behind Joyce, Victoria took a huge intake of breath and gulped as much air into her lungs as possible. From the moment her body had been unzipped out of the body bag she had been taking the most minute breaths, barely taking in enough oxygen to survive but enough to avoid her chest rising enough to avoid detection. She had been lucky that the chemical she had used in her syringes gave her the complexion that she had indeed passed away otherwise she would have been made and she would be sat in a cell right now, instead of the freezing cold metal slab she was laid on.

Slowly rising from her position, Victoria looked around the vicinity for something to use as a weapon. Fortunately for her, Joyce was about to perform an autopsy she there were a multitude of weapons that were at her disposal. Victoria stared at them quickly and without haste reached over, grabbed an instrument, three disposable gloves and put it in the only place that Joyce wouldn't be able to see it straight away. She looked down at the slab and for the marks where she had been laid before and found the exact position she had been in before she had moved.

Victoria knew that now she was able to move, the other signs and symptoms of the chemical would begin to disappear, like the colour of her skin. She knew that she didn't have long to escape once she had killed Joyce so as she breathed normally for a couple of minutes, she thought of an escape plan as quick as she could. The door handle moved and Victoria's breathes became almost none existent again.

Joyce returned into the room mumbling to herself "I knew that's what it looked like but I had to be sure" and placed the headset back on and returned to the computer screen.

Opening her right eye ever so slightly, Victoria peered out of the corner of her eye at Joyce looking at the screen and putting different utensils on a tray next to her. Joyce half turned around which made Victoria close her eyes and return to the slight breathing. She could hear the clinking of metal against other metal, moving of the mouse and the clinking of metal again.

Victoria got the sense that Joyce was now at the foot of the slab looking directly at her and in a hiccup, her eyes were open and her legs were wrapped around Joyce's neck, squeezing them together against her carotid artery. Victoria's hands reached inside of her vagina and pulled out the gloved covered utensil and began removing the gloves on her now diagonally positioned stomach. As they first glove came off Joyce's right hand slammed down into Victoria's chest, just slightly to the left with a pair of rib cutters.

The grip that Victoria's legs had on Joyce's neck immediately ceased and as Joyce withdrew the rib cutters she could see Victoria look up at her. "You don't fool me you fucking bitch, I knew you weren't dead in the hotel room" she said with the highest amount of venom in her voice as the rib cutters plunged into the exact location as the last. As Joyce saw Victoria's body become weaker she walked around the side of the slab and looked into the wound she had made with the rib cutters still sticking out of her chest.

Joyce positioned her hand around the tool, opened them up inside of Victoria's body and looked inside. Her heart was still beating slowly so Joyce reached over at the tray, grabbed a scalpel and sliced the arteries going into Victoria's heart. A couple of unsuccessful pumps of blood later and Victoria's chest cavity was swimming in its own blood pool.

Joyce took off her gloves and reached down to Victoria's thigh and felt for a pulse. She had that position for five minutes until she was more than comfortable that Victoria was dead and released her grip.

Gavin burst through the door with a cordless phone in his hand. All he managed to say before he saw what scene met him in the room was "Wallis is o" and just handed Joyce the phone to her instead of carrying on. Joyce put the phone to her ear and spoke "Hello?"

"Joyce" Wallis said, sounding like he had been in a deep sleep "Victoria isn't dead."

"She is now boss" Joyce replied, hung up and smiled to herself.

Inside of Joyce's head, her one thought was for the revenge of her friends and all of the families that Victoria had killed and affected. *I win you fucking bitch* she thought and played the video over on her computer of Victoria moving when she had left the room, carefully removing the audio where she told Victoria that she knew she wasn't dead in the hotel room.

After all, Joyce loved this job.

Printed in Great Britain
by Amazon